BLUE LINES AND LULLABIES

MILE HIGH SPORTS SERIES

JENNIFER J WILLIAMS

Copyright © 2025 by Jennifer J Williams

All rights reserved.

No part of this book may be reproduced in any form or by any electronic or mechanical means, including information storage and retrieval systems, without written permission from the author, except for the use of brief quotations in a book review.

This book is intended for audiences over the age of 18. It contains mature subject matter. If you do not like steamy sex scenes, adult content, and all the laughs, this book is not for you.

Cover design by KB Barrett Designs

Cover Photography by Lindee Robinson

Cover models: Drew and Hannah

Editing by Brenda Bastien

For Tamara, for only rolling her eyes at me a couple of times when I asked her a million questions about hockey

CHAPTER 1

My back slams unceremoniously against the wall right inside my hotel room door, but I don't even register any pain. Why? Because the man who pushed me into the wall just dropped to his knees in front of me, ready to devour my pussy.

I should back up a few hours, I think.

It's my first night in Denver, Colorado, where I moved to be closer to one of my older brothers. Grant plays for the NHL team here, the Wolves, and he's been pretty miserable since he was traded two seasons ago from our hometown of Portland, Oregon. Grant and I have always been close, and it was an easy decision to follow him to Colorado. Once I found a job, I excitedly packed up all my belongings and started the two-day drive across the Rockies.

Grant volunteered his bare-bones apartment for my first night, but I graciously declined. His mattress is on the floor for crying out loud, and he survives on takeout food and energy drinks. He has barstools, a couch, and the biggest television I've ever seen. If this is where he brings women home, I'd imagine this is also why I haven't heard a thing about any relationships. I bet he doesn't even keep cookable food in the place to make them breakfast after a night of debauchery.

I've read so many stories about athletes and their strict diets, how health-conscious they are, and how they never put processed foods into their bodies. Grant is the exception to that rule, since his diet rivals that of a fifteen-year-old boy going through puberty and eating a family-size bag of pizza rolls every afternoon. It's appalling, and I want no part of that. Don't get me wrong, I love my brother. We have a fantastic sibling relationship, which seems to improve as we age. I can tell Grant anything. But the fact that we barely survived the teenage years living in the same home tells me we shouldn't live together as adults. Plus, most boys are just gross.

I decided to treat myself to a nice hotel on the outskirts of town for a few nights, until I could find an apartment that meets my needs and budget. Is this realistic? No, not really. I'm thankful I have my brother here to fall back on if needed. But I knew I needed to get out of Portland. I just felt so stuck. Stifled. Thirty years old, and I'm starting over in a new state. While I have some savings to ease the pain of no current income, I knew the hotel and meal out would be my last hurrah for a while. And it's just my luck that the most attractive man I've ever seen sat next to me at the restaurant bar next door to my hotel. Devilishly handsome. Dark brown hair with a natural wave that kept falling across his forehead. The deepest brown eyes I'd ever seen. He's quite a bit taller than me, well over six feet, and I quickly had inappropriate visions of what it would be like to be with him.

He told me his name was Gabe, and we got to talking about Colorado. He's also not from here, but he gave me tons of advice on Colorado survival.

"It's crazy windy here. Way windier than you'd think," he said.

I shrugged and rolled my eyes. "It's windy everywhere."

"You'd think that, wouldn't you? But we routinely get hurricane-force winds here."

I'm sorry, what now?

"Oh, and don't rent an apartment, or house, where the parking is on the north side of the building."

"Why?"

"Because the snow won't melt. Ever."

I laughed, thinking he was joking, but his expression never changes. "You're kidding."

"Nope. Tons of memes about it. A tale of two Colorados. South facing buildings have the sun to melt all the snow, so you won't even need to shovel it. Well, most of the time."

"Most of the time?" I remember asking.

He scratched his head in thought. "If it's a blizzard, or we get two or three feet of snow, that changes things."

Holy shit. Feet of snow. *Feet*. Snow in Portland was rare, and hardly ever amounted to more than a couple inches.

"Are you a sports fan?" Gabe asked suddenly, jarring me from my hyper focus on snow.

"Why?" I asked warily. I'm always hesitant to tell anyone about my brother. Grant had already told me the sports fans in Denver were nuts.

"Fans here are pretty rabid for their teams. If you're a fan of another team, I'd suggest keeping quiet about it." I don't say a word about Grant, hockey, or my overall interest in sports. I'm thankful I didn't wear Grant's number twelve Wolves jersey, or any of the other hockey related paraphernalia I've accumulated over the years. I did always think it was cool to wear a jersey with our last name, McNally, on it. Back home, people even call me by Grant's hockey nickname, Nally. But, for all I know, Gabe could be a huge hockey fan, and then he'll try to get me to introduce him. No thank you.

Unfortunately, it wouldn't be the first time a man used me to get to Grant, or his teammates.

I'm the youngest in my family, with all three of my brothers playing professional sports. Honestly, it's a wonder my parents survived all of our childhoods. You'd think we must have some amazing genetics at play, right? Not even close. My father owns an

HVAC company, and my mom is a nurse. And I'm quite possibly the least coordinated woman in the world. I can trip on air. Don't put a set of skates on me and expect it to be successful. Granted, I did play hockey growing up. Since the rest of my siblings were obsessed with sports, I figured I could try one. Hockey was the only sport that excited me. And if I'm stationary, I have excellent aim with the puck. Just don't ask me to move while controlling the stick *and* the puck. And if you want me to throw or kick a ball, don't be mad when it somehow hits you in the face when you weren't even on the field.

I'm digressing.

The more Gabe and I talked as we ate, the more I could feel the sexual chemistry building between us. Our conversations got a little more intimate. We turned toward each other. I touched his hand. He pushed a piece of hair behind my ear. I dragged my fingertip down a line of script on the inside of his arm, and then he put his hand on my thigh.

He's lucky I didn't mount him right there.

When our bills came, and he grabbed mine, I thanked him by asking if he'd like a nightcap in my hotel room. His response of, "I'd fucking love one," will forever be embedded in my memory for how husky and seductive he sounded.

Gabe's lips are on mine before the elevator doors close, and my hands are carving a path along the spectacular back muscles under his shirt soon thereafter. When the doors ding, signaling the arrival at my floor, he unceremoniously throws me over his shoulder before taking off down the hallway.

"Room nine-fourteen," I giggle.

"Get the key ready, or I'm fucking you in the hallway, Firecracker," Gabe grunts as he sprints toward my room. He's called me Firecracker a few times tonight, and I love it more than I thought I would. Typically, I find pet names to be icky, but this seems endearing and cute.

"Why are you calling me Firecracker?" I ask as we arrive at my room, and he puts me back on my feet.

"Because your face lit up more than once when you were talking tonight, and I have a feeling it's going to be fucking spectacular to watch you come," he says against my hair. I stifle a moan as he pulls me back into his body, leaning down to kiss my neck and slide the tip of his tongue against my skin. I shiver and reach up to grab his hair, holding his head against me. My neck is incredibly sensitive, and I love it when men spend time kissing me there once they realize how much I like it. I don't miss the vibration of Gabe's chuckle as he slides a hand around my waist, covering my hand, before dragging it up to wave the keycard in front of the room lock.

Goodness. Gabe teased fucking me in the hallway, and I'm already so far gone that I'd probably have let him. Gabe pushes me gently into the room after I open the door, and once it's closed, I drop my things on the floor and turn into his arms. His lips are on mine immediately, his tongue flicking into my mouth as I wrap my arms around his neck. When his hands finally slide to my ass, he grabs and lifts me, my legs wrapping around his waist.

Moaning, I latch onto his hair as I suck his tongue into my mouth, and Gabe kneads my ass as he spins us to push me against the door. He breaks off the kiss and pants against my cheek. "You can't suck my tongue like that, Firecracker. Makes me want you on your knees right fucking now, with my cock down your throat."

"God, yes," I whimper. I'm not a big fan of blowjobs, but for some reason, I'm aching to taste him.

"Not yet. First time I'm coming, it'll be in this pussy," Gabe growls as he slides a hand between my legs from behind. Looking up at him, I see his lips are puffy. Hooded eyes stare at me fervently as his breathing quickens. I'm only wearing a very thin pair of leggings, and my utterly saturated thong is doing little to conceal how hot and wet I am. "Jesus Christ, Cassie. You're soaked. This all for me, baby?"

For crying out loud. Why is a man calling me baby so damn hot?

Gabe reaches around to grab one ankle, pushing it down so my legs move from his waist. When my feet touch the ground, he drops to his knees. Shit. I've been driving all day. I haven't showered yet. There's no way I'm fresh and ready for oral. "Gabe, no, wait."

He looks up at me, and I can barely see his eyes in the dark room. "If you're about to tell me that you've been on the road all day and you don't want me to get your taste on my tongue, I've got half a mind to throw you over my leg and spank the hell out of you. I don't want to taste fucking soap, Firecracker. I want to taste *you*."

Good God. I may have just come. That is the hottest thing a man has ever said to me. Quite possibly the hottest thing any man has ever said.

I must moan incoherently because Gabe rests his head against my thigh and laughs. "May I continue?"

I'm fairly certain I reply in the affirmative, but it is complete gibberish. Gabe's hands grab the hem of my leggings, pulling them down to my ankles, before helping me to step out of them and my shoes. I'm a heartbeat away from grabbing my thong to remove it as well, but Gabe stops me when he leans forward and tongues my clit through the fabric. At that point, I forget how to breathe.

It's an odd juxtaposition between the wetness of his tongue, and the coarseness of my lace thong against my clit, and it's making me crazy. I don't know what feeling to focus on, and then he slides one finger underneath the fabric to swirl against my opening. Pushing inside, my body clamps down on his digit as he quickly finds my G-spot and rubs against it. I'm two seconds from coming when he leans back slightly, and I cry out in frustration.

"Don't worry, baby. I'll get you there," he whispers as he grabs ahold of the side of my thong and snaps it in half. "Put one leg on my shoulder."

I dutifully follow his order as his thumb finds my engorged button of nerves. I cry out again, this time from pleasure, as Gabe slowly rubs his thumb around and around. Collecting my wetness, he swivels his hand before pushing his thumb against my back hole. I don't have time to think before Gabe latches his lips around my clit, adds a second finger inside my pussy, and pushes his thumb just beyond the ring of muscle. He moans against me as my hands grab his head, and I reflexively begin to move his head how I want him to lick me.

"That's it, baby, use me," he mutters against me, and I feel emboldened, so I push his face further into my pussy. I'm moaning loudly, gyrating against Gabe's face, and I vaguely hear voices outside the door. Stiffening, I move to push Gabe away, but he latches harder on my clit. "Ignore them, Firecracker. Come for me. Give me what's mine."

Sucking my clit again, he nibbles just hard enough to send me into one hell of an orgasm. The triple threat of his tongue, fingers in my pussy, and his thumb in my ass make me erupt in a way I've never experienced before. White-hot pleasure courses through my body, starting at my feet, in a wave that overtakes me, and robs me of the ability to breathe. My knees buckle, and I begin to collapse, but Gabe catches me as he stands.

Three long strides later, we're catapulted onto the bed.

"I figured you would fuck me against the door," I say breathlessly.

"Thought about it. But I prefer having more room to move around. Since you're a good eight inches shorter than me, Firecracker, it could be a feat of physics and prayer for sex against a door. Also, who the hell knows when that door was last cleaned?" Gabe shudders against me dramatically.

"Germaphobe?"

"Sort of. I'm around gross guys a lot. I can't make them be cleaner, though."

I don't ask any further questions. We decided a while ago that we wouldn't share personal information, other than our first names. I think we both know this is a one-night thing. Scratching an itch. I'll never see him again in a city this big.

"How about you stop talking and fuck me?" I ask as I pull his head down to mine. Gabe chuckles against my mouth as he slides his tongue against mine, and I'm pleasantly surprised that I don't hate the taste of myself. Maybe it's a combination of his manly taste with mine, or perhaps I'm just so turned on that I don't care. But a few long kisses later, I'm shimmying against him like a nympho needing another hit of an orgasm.

"Slow down, Firecracker. We've got all night," Gabe says as he bites my nipple through my shirt and bra.

"I'm the most impatient woman you'll ever meet, dammit," I moan.

"I highly doubt that. You strike me as a woman with infinite patience."

He's not wrong. My degree is in early childhood education, and I usually have more patience with children than I do with adults. But right now, my body is taut with feral need, and if he doesn't make me come in the next minute, I'm taking it upon myself to finish the task at hand. Yeah, I had an orgasm against the door. But Gabe makes me want more. Need more. I have this nagging feeling that every orgasm with him will get better.

"I think the next time you come needs to be on my cock," he murmurs. I look at the door, somewhat disappointed that he didn't throw me against it. I read romance books. All the heroes seem to toss their women around. Sex against doors, walls, and even in the shower. When am I going to experience all that? "Fucking hell, Firecracker. You're still thinking about the door."

"I mean, I know I'm not skinny, but you're solid muscle, and I think you could easily hold me against the door," I comment. I have curves. Pockets of flab here and there. I'm not skin and bones, and I never intend to be. I like food too much.

Gabe's head pops up from my chest. "Did you seriously just say you aren't skinny? Jesus, Cassie. Your body is fucking perfect."

"I just meant I'm not tiny."

"What is your definition of tiny?" he asks.

I shrug. "Well, I guess thinner than me. Bony. Easy to pick up and throw around."

Gabe's eyes narrow as he studies me. "Guess you threw down the gauntlet, didn't you?"

"What? No, I didn't throw anything — woah!" I shout as Gabe instantly picks me up and holds me over his head.

"Want me to try it one-handed?" he asks with a devilish glint in his stare.

"Uh, no, I think I'll just give you the benefit of the doubt," I answer hastily. I'd prefer not to have to visit a hospital tonight.

Gabe slowly lowers me until our faces meet, kissing my lips softly. "You really want sex against the door?"

I ponder for a moment. Do I? Honestly, I've never been with someone so virile and strong. I like that Gabe can manhandle me, yet I feel safe and cocooned in this warmth at the same time. And since I'll never see him again, I finally nod. When in Rome. Or maybe it's bite the bullet. Whatever.

Gabe chuckles as he pivots and walks to the door. "You gonna be quiet, or you want to alert the entire floor to what we're doing?"

I hesitate before responding, "I'm not entirely sure."

The answering smile I get is full of fondness, with a cheekiness I didn't expect. I think Gabe wants me to be loud.

"Do you want me to alert the floor to our shenanigans?" I ask incredulously.

"Shenanigans?" he laughs. "Yeah, baby. I think I'd like you to be loud. Bet I can make you really sing."

He did.

Four times.

Gabe

CHAPTER 2

"Are you waiting for an engraved invitation, Daws? Fucking go!" Coach yells.

I thought with Bennett Davenport getting some ass reasonably often, he'd cool off a bit, but I swear it's made him an even bigger jerk of a coach. Not that I'm complaining. I wasn't sad to see Coach Woodward get fired. He was a complete ass; he hated my teammate Luca based on a stupid rumor that Luca was sleeping with Woodward's wife; all the while, he was cheating on his wife with Luca's neighbor. That whole situation was a complete clusterfuck, and I was glad to see him have the door hit him on his way out.

I'm thirty-three years old and have two more years on my contract with the Denver Wolves NHL team. I was traded here a few years ago after spending my entire career in Florida. Hell of a change to go from heat and humidity to oxygen deprivation and zero moisture in the air. Took me about a year to acclimate to the Colorado climate, but I don't hate it. I love being near the mountains, as I'm an avid snowboarder, and I'll never say no to snowmobiling in the Rockies. Plus, there's nothing better than Oktoberfest in Breckenridge. The spectacular mountain views make the hangover worth it.

"Come on, Daws, fucking go," teases the center of my line, Jacob Mitchell. Along with Levi Adamson, we are the first-line forwards for the Wolves. I've spent my entire career at right wing. I thought about being a goalie when I first started playing, but now I know it's not for me. Goalies are just generally weird. They have odd quirks and even more superstitions about the game.

"Shut the fuck up, Jax," I chuckle. A big thing in hockey is getting a nickname, and they are used more often than your actual name. Most are plays on the last name. My last name is Dawson, and I'm called Daws. How the hell Mitchell got Jax as a nickname, I'll never know. And Levi ... well, he either never got a nickname, or refuses to tell us what it is. Generally, nicknames are given out early on in a career. Jax, Levi, and I are all on the tail end of ours. I doubt I'll get any great offers. Plus, I'm just getting tired. There's always a younger and faster shithead coming out of high school who is gunning for my spot.

"Dawson!"

I look over and see the coach motioning for me to skate over to him. "What's up, Coach?"

"Admin is looking for you. You got some important call that came to the main office."

I immediately think the worst. Did something happen to my parents? My sister? I quickly head to the locker room to get cleaned up, then run to the offices at our practice facility.

"Oh, Gabe, you didn't have to run," the secretary admonishes.

"Who called? What was it?" I demand.

"Someone from St. Francis called."

I wrack my brain, trying to think of what she means. "Uh, what?"

"The hospital?"

"Okay?"

"They left a number and asked for you to call back. You'll need to speak with Sandy."

The secretary hands me a number on a small post-it, and I notice it's a local area code. "Oh, it's local."

She looks at me quizzically. "Were you assuming something happened back home?"

I nod. "For someone to try and track me down here, I assumed the worst."

She gives me a kind smile. "I didn't mean to scare you. Call them back. It's most likely nothing."

I say goodbye to her and head out to my car. Whatever this is, I'll deal with it on my way home. I'm tired, and a long soak in my hot tub calls my name.

Many of the guys on the team live close to downtown Denver, but I chose to buy a place on the outskirts of town. I wanted four walls that I didn't have to share with anyone. I grew up in a small condominium, sharing a room with my sister, and I hated every moment of it. But my parents didn't have a lot of money, and we survived as best we could.

I'll never forget the looks on their faces when I bought them a home after my first year in the league. I was able to treat them for a change. They still live in the town I grew up in, a tiny blip on the map in southeastern Ohio. I tried to get them to move to Denver, but they refused.

I plug in Sandy's number at the hospital and pull out of the players' lot behind the practice facility. I'm surprised when someone answers the phone immediately.

"Hi, I'm trying to reach a Sandy? My name is Gabe Dawson."

"Mr. Dawson, yes. I've been trying to reach you about Nicole Givens."

"Uh, ma'am, I don't think I know a Nicole Givens." That name doesn't sound familiar at all. "What is this about?"

"Ms. Givens has been treated here, and she left your name on some paperwork."

Jesus. Probably some puck bunny trying to score some time with me, or some money. It's rarely genuine.

"I'm sorry, but I don't know her. She probably put my name down as a joke or something. I play hockey, and my name is pretty well-known, unfortunately."

"I'm aware of that, Mr. Dawson. We'll still need you to come in and help us with dotting a few i's and crossing a few t's, if that's okay."

I'm beginning to feel a burning sensation at the base of my neck. This can't be good. "Why would I need to come in?"

"Well, there's been a complication, and we need to rectify it."

"What kind of complication? Can you forward me to this chick's room? Let me speak to her, and I'll see if I can figure out if I actually know her."

"We can't do that, Mr. Dawson."

"Why not?"

Sandy sighs into the phone. "Sir, Ms. Givens had a rare complication. I'm unable to discuss it over the phone. Are you able to come in?"

Dammit. I can hear my hot tub crying my name right now. "I guess."

"I'll see you soon."

Thirty minutes later, I'm checking into the valet parking at a hospital in a less-than-ideal part of Denver. I'm apprehensive about leaving my truck here. Oh well. That's why I have auto insurance.

Finding my way to Sandy's office, I'm surprised when it's down a long and stark hallway. As I find the office number Sandy texted to me after our conversation, I notice the sign above the door says "bereavement." I'm momentarily stupefied because I can't remember what that word means.

"Mr. Dawson?" A middle-aged woman stares expectantly at me from a small desk inside the office. "Please come in."

As soon as I step into her office, I realize what bereavement means. It means death. "Oh, shit. She died, didn't she? This Nicole chick died."

"Yes. I'm sorry to have to tell you this, Mr. Dawson."

I move to sit in the chair opposite her desk. "I really don't know why I'm here then if she's dead. Did she list me as the person to pay her medical bills or something?"

"No, she had medical insurance. That's not the problem. You see, Mr. Dawson, Ms. Givens suffered a rare complication while undergoing a cesarean section that proved to be fatal. Doctors tried relentlessly to bring her back, but she couldn't be saved."

"Cesarian? That's giving birth, right?"

"Yes."

"Did the baby survive?"

"Yes. A little girl. She's being monitored, but she suffered no ill effects from the birth."

"Oh, that's good." I let out a small exhale, relieved for at least one piece of good news. "I still don't get why I'm here —"

Oh my fucking God.

Time slows to a crawl. The clock above Sandy's head slowly ticks; each time the second hand moves, my brain pulses.

Nicole Givens.

"Nicole is blonde, right? Was blonde. Blue eyes, I think? Star tattoo on her shoulder." Suddenly, my memory is crystal clear. She wasn't a puck bunny, but someone I met at a bar outside of town, and with whom I had spent one night.

"Yes."

"Is the kid mine?"

"That's what we're hoping to find out. We'd like you to take a DNA test."

"How did you find me? I mean, how?"

"She listed you in the paperwork when she came in for her induction."

I can feel the blood pulsing through my veins, my heart beating so hard I bet it's visible on the outside. Am I a dad? How is this fucking possible? "She had — I used a condom. And she said she was on the pill."

"No birth control is one hundred percent, Mr. Dawson."

"Why the fuck am I just finding out about this now? She fucking lives here! She could have told me months ago! I would have been here, could have been here when ..." I trail off. I don't know what I would have done. And now I'll never understand why she chose not to tell me about my daughter.

My daughter.

"Can I see her? The baby?"

"Yes. I'd first like you to sign off on these bereavement papers so I can relinquish Ms. Givens' personal belongings to you, and then we'll get the paternity test completed."

"Shouldn't her stuff go to someone who knew her? Parents or something?"

"Ms. Givens said her parents passed on many years ago. She didn't speak of any friends, but nurses said she was very excited about becoming a mom."

Jesus Christ. I can't believe this.

Two hours and a DNA test later, I'm whisked into the neonatal intensive care unit, where I'm immediately told to scrub my hands and arms up to my elbows, then asked to suit up in a paper gown, hair net, and booties.

"I thought you said the baby was fine?" I ask nervously as I slide the booties over my shoes.

"This is more of a precaution. She's passed every test so far, which is excellent news," Sandy tells me kindly.

She motions for me to walk into a sequestered room, where I can see individual spaces with incubators. Suddenly, I feel like my feet are encased in concrete. I'm sluggishly trailing behind Sandy as she steadily walks toward the furthest incubator.

I'm about to meet a baby that might be mine.

Holy shit.

"It's okay, Mr. Dawson. Take all the time you need," Sandy says quietly, smiling warmly as she stands next to the incubator. I swallow hard and force myself to take the final few steps to stand beside her.

Looking down, I'm momentarily unable to breathe.

I know immediately she's mine. How do I know? Gut feeling. Instinct. Whatever.

I can't take my eyes off of her. She's wrapped tightly in a blanket, a hat on her tiny head, but I can see a bit of dark hair peeking out from under the hat. As if she knows I'm here, her eyes suddenly open, and she looks at me. I feel that look in the depths of my soul. I'm connected to this breathtaking baby girl, and it's as if my life is actually starting, right at this moment. Everything changes.

"Would you like to hold her?"

"Yes," I breathe. Pant is a better explanation for my breathing, if I'm being honest. My heart is racing as I wring my hands together nervously.

Sandy motions for me to sit in the rocking chair behind me, then opens the incubator to carefully pick up the baby. I hear a little cry as she's moved, and I immediately pop up from the chair, ready to protect her. How dare Sandy hurt my daughter!

Jesus. Dad mode came on pretty fast.

"Is she okay?" I finally say, hovering behind Sandy.

"She's fine. Newborns make all kinds of noises, Mr. Dawson. You'll need to get used to that, I think."

"I'm sorry. This is so surreal, and I don't know how to act right now," I confess.

"You're doing just fine. You're acting like a dad," she says with a smile. "Sit back down, and I'll put her in your arms."

Once seated, the most beautiful thing I've ever seen is placed in my arms, and it's as if time stops. Her eyes connect with mine again, and I notice she has my nose. Her eyes are a dark blue, nothing like mine, and I can't remember the color of her mom's eyes. I think they were blue, but I'm not sure.

"Can you, uh, can you tell me what color her mom's eyes are? I mean, were. I think Nicole had blue eyes, but I'm second-guessing my memories now," I murmur.

"Babies aren't born with their final eye color. It'll slowly change over the next few months. A baby's eyes lack pigment, so many appear to have blue, or gray, eyes. But if you'd really like to know, I can try to track down the information."

I look up at Sandy and nod. "I would, actually. If I am her father, I want to be able to tell her more about her mother."

Sandy's smile falters as she nods. "I'll see what I can find out for you."

"Are you allowed to tell me what happened to her mother?" I ask weakly.

Sandy sighs, and grabs a chair to pull up beside me. "I'm not at liberty to discuss explicit details, as you aren't technically immediate family to Ms. Givens, but I can tell you it was a spontaneous issue that developed immediately after birth. Ms. Givens developed a hemorrhage, and the doctors couldn't stop the bleeding."

"So she saw the baby at least?" I ask hopefully.

"She did."

"Ha — had she picked a name out?" I stammer.

"I believe she did. Let me look at the file," Sandy says as she pulls out an iPad. A few moments later, she nods affirmatively. "Mackenzie. I don't know a middle name, unfortunately."

"Mackenzie," I whisper, and the baby's eyes immediately open as if she knows that is her name. "Hi, sweet girl."

"The paternity test should be ready by the end of the day," Sandy whispers. "I know you'll want to know as quickly as possible."

"I didn't know it could happen that fast," I admit.

"At-home tests take longer. When it's done at a hospital, we can put a rush on the results."

I'm already attached to this little girl, and I don't know how I'll react if she isn't mine.

Four hours later, I'm officially a dad.

"I assume you'll need some time to get your home ready for a baby, but we have a few things here we can give you. You'll need a car seat, crib or bassinet, formula, and bottles."

"That's it?" I ask incredulously.

Sandy chuckles. "It's not *it*, but it's all you really need to start. We'll give you some clothes, diapers, and burp cloths. We can also list things you'll want to accumulate over the next few weeks."

"Live-in help would be at the top of the list," I murmur. Fucking hell. It's the middle of hockey season. I have no idea how I'm going to handle this when we have a road trip in a little over a week. I haven't even notified the coaching staff yet. "When do I get to take her home?"

"We're running some repeat tests tomorrow to ensure she's as perfect as we think she is. Then, as long as you have a car seat installed, you're welcome to take her home tomorrow afternoon. I need to finish some paperwork, but you can stay here until visiting hours are over at eight."

As soon as Sandy leaves, my phone vibrates in my pocket. Shit. It's Grant, my teammate.

"Yo, douche-canoe! Thought we were having dinner tonight," he shouts.

"Jesus, man. Keep your voice down," I hiss.

"Why? Shit, Daws, are you getting an afternoon delight? Hey, puck bunny! He's got the herp, so make sure he wraps it up!" Grant yells.

Grant's voice carries, and I watch in misery as Mackenzie's face screws up as if she's in pain. The guttural cry that releases from her tiny body is surprising.

"What the hell was that?" Grant whispers. "If that's a puck bunny, I'm calling the cops."

"No puck bunny. I just found out I have a daughter," I mutter.

"No fucking way!" he shouts.

"Grant, I swear to God, if you shout one more fucking time, I'm coming through this phone and muzzling your ridiculous ass!" I growl.

"Damn. Sorry, bro. A baby? Seriously? With whom?" he asks.

"A chick I met at a bar about 10 months ago, I think."

"You think? You don't remember her?"

I sigh. "I vaguely remember her. It was one night, and we didn't exchange numbers. I provided the rubber, so I know this wasn't a get-rich-quick scheme."

"Just ask her, dude. She'll tell you where you met."

"I can't."

"Why not?"

"She died right after giving birth, man."

"Oh fuck," Grant whispers.

"I don't know what I'm going to do. I have nothing, and I'm supposed to take her home tomorrow. They said I need a crib, a car seat, and formula? And how the fuck am I supposed to do this when we go on the road?"

"You're set on doing this, right? Doing the dad thing?"

"Yeah," I tell him. "Yes, absolutely. I took one look at her, and I knew she was mine. I couldn't give her up."

"What's her name?"

"Mackenzie. The staff said that's what her mom wanted to name her, so I'm sticking with that."

"Mackenzie Dawson. Sounds pretty dope."

Damn. It really does.

"Listen. Call Coach. He needs to hear this first. Then, get the group chat going. We'll get you hooked up. You staying at the hospital all night?"

"They said I can only stay until visiting hours are over."

Grant guffaws. "Please. You and I both know you just have to look at whatever nurse tries to kick you out and give her those puppy dog eyes of yours. They'll let you stay."

I quietly chuckle. "You're probably right."

"Does your front door still have the same code to get in?"

"Yeah, why?"

"I've got an idea. You want a crib in your room, or in one of your spare rooms?"

"My room, I guess. I don't know. Is there protocol for this?" I ask exasperatedly.

"Not sure. Ask your mom, then text me the answer. I'll handle the rest. Gotta go!"

"Wait, what the hell do you mean? Grant? Grant!" I pull the phone away from my ear to see he's already ended the call, and I'm not sure if I should be happy, or scared, about whatever he may do to my house while I'm not there.

CHAPTER 3

"What the hell happened here?" I ask incredulously. After zero sleep at the hospital, I'm horribly exhausted. Grant was right, though. One pitiful look, and the nurses turned a blind eye to my refusal to leave the NICU. I'm not sure if I would have slept anyway. I spent an hour on the phone with my parents. My mom sobbed incoherently more than once, forcing my incredibly ill-equipped father to deal with her *and* keep the conversation moving with me. I know my dad loves his kids, but he's not the most verbal man out there. It was like pulling teeth while my mom attempted to get herself together.

With a massive bag of hospital donations strapped to my back, I've got Mackenzie still strapped in her car seat as I attempt to lumber into my house. At least, I think this is my house. It looks like the baby section of Target just blew up in here.

"I had nothing to do with this," I hear from my right, and I turn to see my teammate Luca Santo. Luca and I got off on the wrong foot, but we've established a ceasefire.

"If you didn't do this, why are you here?" I ask before hearing a disturbance coming from the living room.

Luca sighs. "They made me come."

I'm about to ask who 'they' is, but the disturbance comes into view. Grant, Levi, and Jax move into the kitchen as I carefully set the car seat on the island. I'm already exhausted, and the only thing I did was drive her home.

"You wash the sheets before you put them on the mattress, ass face," Levi shouts.

"What does it fucking matter? It's a baby. She won't know the difference," Jax argues. I see the sheet they're both holding, with Grant evidently playing referee in the middle of this unneeded tug-of-war in my house.

"Guys, lower your voices before you wake her —" I don't get to finish my thought before a loud cry fills the air. "Dammit."

"Fuck, man. Sorry," Jax says sheepishly, scratching his curly light brown hair.

"Why is she crying? Does she need a bottle? Or to be changed?" Levi asks. When I cock an eyebrow at him, he shrugs, and his brown locks fall haphazardly over his forehead. "I've got four little sisters, man. I was changing diapers before I hit double digits."

Grant shakes his head and chuckles. The move seems oddly familiar, making me pause to study him. I've seen that move before. And not on him.

It means a lot to me that these three guys are here — well, and I guess Luca, too — because I don't have a fucking clue what I'm doing. As I painstakingly unhook the car seat straps, and gently pick up Mackenzie, I hear an "aw" from at least one of the guys.

"Damn, dude. You're a dad," Grant says quietly.

Mackenzie stops crying as soon as I pick her up and settle her into the crook of my arm, choosing instead to look around at her new surroundings. "I am a dad. Now, can one of you numb nuts explain what the hell happened here?"

Grant chuckles. "Well, when you didn't activate the amazing phone tree, I did it. All the guys started asking me questions to which I had no answers, so I had my sister help me set up a registry for you at Target. The whole team bought it out in a few hours, and boxes started arriving early this morning. We were trying to get everything set up before you got home, but these two decided to argue about the fucking crib sheets, so here we are."

I look around, bewildered, at the stacks of things on my counters. Boxes are strewn everywhere. "And I'll need all of this?"

"Well, my sister suggested we add some things to the registry for a little further down the road. So you've got a variety of diaper sizes, plus all kinds of clothes going up to twelve months. She also suggested we add a bunch of different pacifiers because apparently, babies are fickle about what kind of ... uh, nipple they like." Grant's face turns red as he finishes the final statement.

I feel movement in my arms, and I look down to see Mackenzie turn toward my chest and open her mouth. "Damn. She's already hungry."

"How do you know?" Jax asks with wide eyes.

"The nurses told me it's called rooting when the baby turns toward you and tries to find a food source."

"Huh," Jax says as he watches Mackenzie.

"Can someone take her so I can get a bottle ready?" I ask. Jax and Grant step backward while Levi rolls his eyes.

"Jesus. I'll take her," he says.

Before he can pick her up, Luca steps forward. "Uh, actually, can I take her? I, uh, need a little practice?"

We all stare at him. I smile broadly as realization sets in. "Santzy, are you telling us you knocked up your girl?"

He smiles reluctantly. "I'm neither confirming, nor denying, that my girl is pregnant."

"By all means, you need some practice," I tell him as I gently deposit her into his arms. Luca is like a brick wall. He looks remarkably out of place with a tiny baby in his arms, but the look of wonderment on his face as he stares down at my daughter is dazzling.

Opening up the bag of goodies the nurses sent me home with, I remove the canister of formula, a bottle of water, and a baby bottle. Then I whip out my phone to pull up my notes.

"What are you doing?" Levi asks.

"I took notes. I want to be sure I do this correctly," I mutter.

"Fucking hell. Give me the damn bottle, Daws. You don't need notes." Levi grabs the baby bottle and water. "Newborns don't drink much. Start with two ounces. Never put the formula in first. Always start with the water, then add the formula."

"In the hospital, they warmed the bottle up slowly," I comment, and Levi shrugs.

"Pretty sure there's a bottle warmer in one of the boxes, but for now, she'll be fine drinking it at room temperature. Don't microwave it because there can be pockets of super-hot water that can burn her mouth." Levi expertly measures out the water and formula and has the bottle ready for Mackenzie in a matter of moments. He looks at me expectantly. "You gonna feed her, or should I?"

"Uh, you?" I say hesitantly. Levi seems pretty confident in his baby abilities, and I kind of want to see him continue. He snatches Mackenzie out of Luca's arms, grabs what he tells me is a burp cloth off the counter, and walks out of the kitchen. The rest of us file quietly behind him.

"Did you guys rearrange?" I ask, noticing my couches are on different walls.

"Yeah, because the only place we could put the rocking chair was right by the window, and we worried the sun would come in and hurt her eyes. Oh, there's another rocking chair in your bedroom. Babies get up a lot at night," Levi murmurs.

Wow. They really thought of everything.

"The coaches chipped in and got you a crib, so we put that in the bedroom next to yours. But we also got a bassinet, and that's in your room," he continues.

I flop on the couch closest to Levi and Mackenzie and rub my eyes. "I don't know how the fuck I'm going to do this. Coach said I can take the next ten days off. He's listing me as a healthy scratch, and telling the media it's a personal matter, or a family emergency. My mom and dad want to visit, but they can't just leave their jobs, so they're planning to visit over spring break. That's six weeks from now. What the fuck am I supposed to do?"

Grant clears his throat. "I may have a solution for you."

"I'm all ears."

"Well, my sister just moved here from Oregon. She wanted a change, so she came here without a job lined up. She has a background in early childhood education, and she's the one who helped me with the registry. I think she'd be a great live-in nanny for you."

"Live-in nanny?" I ask.

"Honestly, it makes more sense that way. Rather than you dropping Mackenzie off somewhere, she stays here. When you're gone, my sister will be here for whatever Mac needs. Plus, my sister doesn't have an apartment lined up, so you'd be helping her out."

"That's true. And don't call my daughter Mac."

"It's a nickname, Daws. Surely you understand a nickname."

"You can call her Mackenzie or Kenzie. Once she's old enough to approve her own nicknames, you may ask her if she is okay with you calling her Mac."

"That's fair," Grant says with a chuckle. He grabs his phone and fires off a message. "My sister is actually at a coffee shop a couple miles away. I can have her stop by so you can interview her and see if it'll be a good fit."

I watch as Levi begins patting Mackenzie on the back, and immediately, she lets out a massive belch, making all the guys laugh. "Yeah, please do. If I could get someone on board immediately, it would really help me out with one less thing to worry about."

"Alright. I'll let Cassie know to head over."

Cassie?

No. Just a coincidence.

It can't be the girl from the restaurant.

I shake off a shiver as I grab my daughter and bury my nose in the side of her face.

"Hey, Daws! Get your ass down here and meet the nanny!" Grant calls from downstairs. I've gone up to check out the crib and changing table the guys put together. Fortunately, my main bedroom is spacious, and I only had a bed, two nightstands, and a dresser. Adding two pieces of furniture makes it slightly cramped but still doable.

Mackenzie used the opportunity of being in her new space to take a massive dump in her diaper. How can babies poop this much? It can't be normal. It just went everywhere, and I'm definitely going to need a lot of practice on diaper changes. Something tells me this little girl will give me as many opportunities as I need.

As I descend the staircase, I hear a light, airy, female voice giggling at something Jax says, and my hackles go up. That voice. I've heard it. I've felt it on my skin. And I'm suddenly furious that Jax is hearing it, too. Turning the corner, I see my one-night stand surrounded by my teammates, basking in the glory of all their attention. Now I'm pissed.

I clear my throat, angry that Cassie is enjoying their attention, and I'm ready to tell Grant it won't work. No way. I'm still ticked that I went to get us breakfast the morning after we met, and when I returned, she had completely checked out of the hotel. I even asked if she left a note for me, and the front desk staff was apologetic when they confirmed she hadn't. I didn't want it to be just one night. I wanted more. She rocked my world that night, and not a day has gone by that I haven't thought about her.

Looking at her now, I'm remembering every minute detail. Having her long blonde hair wrapped around my fist. How her delicate fingers felt scratching along my back. How fucking phenomenal every curve of her luscious body felt against mine, and especially her hazel eyes filled with lust as she watched me come inside her. It was a night I'll never forget. But why did she run?

When Cassie's eyes meet mine, I see a momentary spark of joy in her gaze until her eyes narrow to slits and her lips purse into a straight line. She clears her throat before grabbing her bag from the side table and putting it on her shoulder. "I'm sorry, Grant, but this won't work. I know him. It's a hard no."

"What? You know him? How? You've been here all of ten seconds, Cass," Grant sputters.

"Two weeks, actually," I blurt out. Yeah, I know. It sounds pitiful, even to me. But I haven't stopped thinking about her, and now Cassie is standing in my home, and she has the audacity to look pissed at *me*. "You've got a lot of nerve to be standing in my house and looking at me like I'm the villain here."

Cassie's mouth drops open in shock. "I have nerve? Seriously? When I woke up, you were gone! You didn't even leave your number or anything!"

"Shit," Jax grumbles, but I soldier on.

"I went to get breakfast for you, Firecracker. I was gone less than an hour, and when I got back, you had already checked out. I asked the front desk staff if you had left me a number or note, and you hadn't left either."

"A whole hour to get breakfast?" Levi asks.

I turn to him and shrug. "Denver Biscuit Company. I figured she hadn't had it before. There was a line, and it took a while."

"Ah. That makes sense. It really is good food, Cass," Levi says with a smirk.

"Hey!" Grant interjects. "Nobody calls her Cass except me. Now, I'd like to know how the two of you apparently met before I even saw you when you got here!"

Cassie sighs before turning to him. "I stayed in a hotel one night. Remember? I'd been traveling all day, and I just wanted my own space before I would be in yours for an unknown amount of time. I went next door to a restaurant and sat at the bar. Gabe sat next to me."

Grant turns to me, his expression murderous. "What the fuck were you doing at a restaurant by her hotel?"

Jostling Mackenzie as I reposition her on my shoulder, I reply, "I'm allowed to have dinner out, Nally. Considering I'm not even sure you mentioned your sister moving here, I doubt you can assume there are some nefarious plans going on here. Complete coincidence, trust me."

"Well," Cassie says with a haughty laugh, "maybe you should have been home instead, since clearly you weren't supposed to be out that night anyway." She makes a pointed look down at my daughter.

"Oh, sis, um, that's not exactly true —" Grant begins, but I hold up a hand to stop him.

"Let her think what she wants. She decided about me as soon as she saw me come down the stairs. Do you want the job or not?"

"I think I already said no, jerk face," she retorts.

"Jerk face? Is that the best you can do?" I ask.

"No, but I'm not going to say what I really think in front of a child."

I lean toward her in a mocking manner before whispering, "Pretty sure she won't be repeating things for a bit, so by all means, say what you want to say."

Cassie's face reddens as her hands clenched tightly into fists. "Fine, asshole. You want me to be honest? You're just a typical hockey fuck boy. You do whatever you want, and you don't think about any repercussions. I bet you wouldn't even be in that little girl's life if her mom hadn't passed away. You take and take and take. I feel pity for your daughter, and that she'll have to grow up with *you* as a father."

I feel the blood drain out of my face as I reflect on her words. It's so quiet we can hear interstate traffic from a mile away. Grant looks miserably at me, unsure of how to speak. Jax has a minor smirk on his face, and Levi is shooting fiery glances between me and Cassie.

Cassie looks momentarily chagrined as she attempts to speak. "That was unnecessary. I was out of line, and —"

"No," I interrupt. "You made your point. Best if you stop talking now. I'm going upstairs. Let yourselves out, please."

I grab the hospital bag with everything I'll need for Mackenzie, then make my way back up the stairs.

What she said isn't too far off what most people think about professional athletes as a whole. People definitely think similar thoughts about hockey guys. And I'm sure there have been times when I've fit that mold with horrifying accuracy. But it had been months since I'd slept with anyone. Hell, Nicole might have been the last one-night stand I had. I dated someone briefly for about a month. It was apparent we were on different pages, and we separated amicably.

As I quietly close my bedroom door, I hear Grant yelling at Cassie. "This was the perfect job for you, Cass, and your mouth just had to go and fuck it up! He was going to let you live here rent-free!"

We hadn't actually discussed the rent, but I probably would have let her.

Three hours later, I wish I had begged Cassie to stay. Mackenzie hasn't stopped crying, and I'm at a loss as to what to do. I called my mom, and she began crying when she heard her granddaughter. I hung up when I realized she wasn't in any way able to help when she appeared to be hysterical at the same time.

I'd changed her, fed her, changed her again, tried on three

different outfits of differing fabrics to see if one possibly irritated her, and then began pacing back and forth across my bedroom. I hadn't thought about the outfits being an issue, but Levi suggested it. He wasn't too thrilled when I called him for the fourth time, but he patiently walked me through what he remembered from the newborn stage. The only thing that seemed to settle her down was the constant movement, patting her diapered tush, and humming Britney Spears songs. Kenzie apparently has an affinity for *...Baby, One More Time*, because that settles her down immediately. I'm deep in a rousing rendition for the sixth or seventh time, so I don't hear my bedroom door open. When I turn and see an outline of a body, I jump and yell simultaneously, frightening my daughter and making her cry again.

"Oh, shoot," a female voice says fretfully. "I'm sorry, I didn't mean to scare you, and make her cry."

"Shh, shh, shh," I whisper in Kenzie's ear. "It's okay, sweet girl. I've got you. Daddy's got you." When she settles back down, I turn and glare at a remorseful Cassie. "What the hell are you still doing here?"

"Grant wouldn't let me leave," she blurts out. "He said I needed to apologize to you, that I didn't know the whole story, and that I'd misjudged you."

"He left you here?" I ask incredulously.

"No, he's asleep on your couch. He said he'd wait me out, because I was being a stubborn ass."

"He's not wrong," I mutter. I see her staring at Kenzie's diapered bottom, and my brow furrows in confusion. "Is there an issue?"

"Hmm?" Cassie asks.

"Why are you staring at her diaper?"

"Oh, I'm not staring at her diaper. It's just ... you're not wearing a shirt," Cassie stammers.

"And?"

"Well, why aren't you wearing one? You're making me uncomfortable."

"You barged into my bedroom uninvited, and you have the audacity to tell me you're uncomfortable? That's rich," I laugh. "It's skin-to-skin. The nurses said Mackenzie would like it. It's the only thing that is settling her down right now."

"Have you tried swaddling?" Cassie asks.

"Is that when they look like a baby burrito?"

Cassie giggles, and it reminds me of the Cassie I first met. "Yes, like a burrito. Swaddling puts pressure on the entire body, which makes babies feel like they're back in the womb. It's comforting to most, but some babies hate it."

"She seemed to like it in the hospital," I murmur.

"Can I try?" Cassie asks softly, and I nod. "Let me wash my hands before I handle her. May I use your sink?"

I point her toward the en suite bathroom and wait for her to return. Cassie gingerly takes Mackenzie from my arms and easily slides her into a hold that looks remarkably like carrying a football. Kenzie's arms and legs dangle from Cassie's arm, but her head is held protectively in Cassie's hand.

Cassie rummages in the hospital bag and pulls out a simple white blanket. I watch as she lays the blanket out on my bed, then pulls down one edge to make a triangle. She places Kenzie in the middle, then folds the edges snugly to make the burrito. Mackenzie immediately stops crying.

"What kind of sorcery was that?" I blurt out. Cassie picks Mackenzie up and snuggles her against her chest.

"No sorcery. I can teach you how to do it." She motions like she's going to take Kenzie out of the burrito, and I throw up my hands to stop her.

"Don't you dare. She's quiet and happy. You can teach me another time."

"Okay," she says with a light giggle. She hands Kenz to me, and I stare down at my daughter in complete awe.

"I don't know what I did to deserve her, but I'm so fucking

thankful she's here. How is it possible to love someone so much when you've just met them?" I ask.

Cassie reaches up to touch Kenzie's cheek lightly, her thumb caressing Kenzie's cheek in reverence. "I only just met her, and I'm already half in love with her, so I'm not sure I can answer that question objectively."

"Please be her nanny. Seriously. Grant wouldn't have recommended you if you weren't the best for the job."

"You haven't even interviewed anyone else. How can you say I'm the best?"

"I don't know," I whisper. "Gut instinct, I guess."

"Is it ..." Cassie hesitates.

"What?"

"Will it be weird? Me being here? It's bad enough I had to basically tell my brother I had a one-night stand, but then to find out it's not only his teammate, but also the single dad I would be nannying for? It's a lot, Gabe."

I'll ignore the shiver that threatens to dance up my spine when she says my name. She rarely said my name during our night together. "It will only be weird if we allow it. I'm not going to lie, I wanted to see you again. I did go back to the hotel, Cass. I didn't intend for that to be our only time together. But now, things are different. My focus has to be on my daughter."

"I know," she whispers. "For what it's worth, I wanted to see you again, too. Maybe not like this, though."

"I'd like to offer you the job. We can take it on a conditional basis, and make sure we're both comfortable moving forward. We have one last road trip before the playoffs start, and maybe we won't even make it far. I may only need you for a month or two."

Cassie studies me, her eyes dancing between mine. "And you'd want me to live here? For the time being?"

"Yes, I think that would be best. It sounds like it would also help you as you get settled."

Cassie shudders. "I need out of Grant's house before I murder him, or any of his random puck bunnies."

I stifle a laugh. "Problems?"

"Yes!" she hisses. "I found a strange woman in my bedroom this morning, and *she* yelled at *me*! She thought I was another puck bunny!"

"Grant does have a revolving door," I chuckle. For a while, he was in a relationship, and we all thought he'd be proposing soon. Then suddenly, he became the team ho, and wouldn't answer any questions about his girlfriend.

"Is that something I'll encounter here as well?" she asks bluntly.

"No. Especially not with Mackenzie here, but I've never been a big proponent of the puck bunny scene. I prefer to have a connection with someone."

"Okay."

"Okay?"

"Yeah. I'll take the job. And the room."

I let out a big exhale. "Oh, thank fuck."

A loud grunt fills the air, followed by a disgusting gurgle, and then a horrendous odor. Cassie lets out a harmonious giggle. "I'll leave you to it, Daddy."

"I guess you start tomorrow then, huh," I call out as she opens my bedroom door and skips down the hall.

"We can discuss a dirty diaper stipend tomorrow."

Nice.

Cassie

CHAPTER 4

I've never had good luck. I know some people say they don't have any luck, but mine is usually just bad luck. I'm typically a rule follower, but nearly every time I break a rule, I suffer the consequences almost immediately. It's like that Alanis Morissette song, *Isn't It Ironic*. If I run a red light, I'll get pulled over. If something accidentally gets buried underneath another item as I leave a bulk store, I'll be selected for a random search at the door. So it really shouldn't have surprised me that the *one* time I had a one-night stand, it turned out to be a teammate of my brother's, *and* the guy who needed me to be a nanny to his newborn daughter.

I was furious when I woke up that morning, and Gabe was nowhere to be found. I thought we had a connection, and I felt so used. Humiliated. Angry. Horribly self-conscious. Was I not any good? Was he that repulsed by my body, or our chemistry? I spent the last two weeks dissecting every tiny detail from that night, wondering what went wrong. Finding out he wanted to surprise me with breakfast, and came back to find me gone, was so on brand for me and my ridiculous bad luck with men.

So now I have to keep it professional. Try not to drool over him when he's being so dang adorable with Mackenzie. Or fawn over him when he walks around shirtless, which I learned immediately is what he normally does. As if I didn't have the memory of his pecs tattooed in my brain, now I see them multiple times a day because *the man does not keep a shirt on.*

He really took it to heart that whole 'skin-to-skin' thing. Mackenzie seems to quiet down as soon as she's resting on his heart, and I can't say I blame her.

I'm not completely complaining, but it's like shopping without your wallet. I've touched the merchandise, but now I can't look at, or touch it, again. It's brutal.

By the third day, I began lowering my gaze whenever Gabe walked into my line of vision. I'd make eyes at Mackenzie and act like Gabe didn't exist. I figured it might be awkward and uncomfortable if I asked him, *again,* to put a shirt on. What am I allowed to do here? I don't hate the view. But it makes me think ... things. Things I shouldn't be thinking about my employer. Rather than open it up to discussion, I'm averting my eyes.

I have to hand it to the guys on the hockey team. They really showed up for Gabe. Mackenzie will want for nothing anytime soon. There must be over one thousand diapers stacked against a wall, next to dozens of boxes of wipes. Two cabinets full of formula, bottles, burp cloths, and pacifiers. Gabe's entire refrigerator is stuffed to the brim with food for him. Quite a few frozen meals, lots of protein drinks, and a ridiculous amount of cheese. The last time my brother stopped by, he whispered that Gabe loves cheese, and it's a snack he keeps on hand. Evidently he has a tiny cooler for away trips, and packs himself some slices for the plane.

My first test came when Gabe ran a couple of errands by himself, leaving me with Mackenzie for the first time. The sweet girl is still a little unsure of things, and fusses anytime I sit down, so I roam Gabe's house while patting Mackenzie's bottom constantly.

"Your daddy is insanely organized," I murmur as I take a gander at his pantry. Is there something in the water at ice rinks?

Every hockey player I've ever met has a system for their homes. It's rare that I find one who isn't regimented in some aspect of their daily life. My brother has an odd appetite, sure. But he has every inch of his place organized down to the millimeter. He's like Monica on *Friends*: if I move a pillow even a half inch over, *he will know*.

After putting Kenzie down for her nap in Gabe's room, I catch myself loitering near the large walk-in closet. I've never been inside, and the pull to snoop is very enticing. Quietly pushing open the door, I take a quick inhale as I survey the space. This closet is a dream.

Large built-ins cover every wall in a beautiful white oak color, and a massive island with a marble top sits in the middle of the space. Gabe has spread his clothes out to cover all the space, but it's clear this closet is meant for two people. I take a hesitant step inside, and lights go on underneath the cabinetry automatically, making me gasp as I quickly shut the door so the lights don't wake Kenzie up. Crap. Now I'm really in here. If Gabe walks in, I have no valid excuse. Oh well.

Taking a look around, I notice his attention to detail and the art of organization. Matching drawers enclose carefully rolled up ties, matched socks, and folded boxer briefs. A large drawer full of perfectly folded T-shirts makes me giggle, knowing the drawer in my room has every article of clothing haphazardly shoved in there.

Suits line one wall, organized in an ombré rainbow of color. I drag my finger down a particularly beautiful suit in burgundy, thinking how amazing it must look on Gabe's form. I bet all of these suits look gorgeous on him. As I round the island, I find a drawer full of colognes, and I can't fight the desire to smell each and every one of them until I get a whiff of the one he wore on our night together.

"There it is," I sigh, as I take a deep breath against the sprayer. I wonder if he'd notice if I took it. I'd love to spray my pillow with it. A maniacal giggle bursts from my mouth as I realize how nuts that sounds. I'm debating on stealing my boss's cologne so I can use some of it in secret. Good God.

I'll just buy my own bottle.

"Holy shit, Givenchy? That has to be expensive," I murmur, whipping out my phone to look up the price. I have a mini heart attack when I see how much it costs. "Two hundred bucks? Absolutely not!"

Nope, we're back to stealing my boss's cologne. I'm not dropping that much money on male cologne. The most I'd have spent would be around fifty. Maybe even less.

"Cass?"

Shit. Gabe is home, and I'm creeping like a crazy person in his closet! Quickly exiting the closet, I make it to Gabe's bedroom door as he reaches it from the other side.

"Shh," I whisper, quietly closing the door behind me. "I just put her down. She's been a little fussy this morning."

"Fuck," he says sullenly. "I was hoping to give her a bottle before her nap."

I fight the urge to smile as I watch Gabe pout. "You'll have so many more opportunities to feed your daughter, Gabe."

"I know," he sighs. "I hope it never gets old. I hope I always want to spend every moment with her."

"I think it's a choice people make. You can either choose to be positive, and recognize that children grow up fast, or you can think about all the things you feel you're missing out on from before you became a parent. I like that you're all in with fatherhood. It looks good on you." I stop, suddenly embarrassed at my gushing over Gabe, and feel my cheeks heat.

"Thanks, Cass. That means a lot," he responds quietly. "Want to come downstairs and have some lunch?"

"Sure." I silently follow Gabe back down the stairs, trying desperately not to stare at his ass. He's got an exceptional derriere.

"You alright with a salad with smoked salmon?" Gabe asks, and my mouth waters.

"Sounds amazing," I confess. "Did you make it yourself?"

"No," he laughs. "I have a catering company that prepares meals for a lot of the local athletes. I always order double so I have leftovers. Usually I take the salmon from this salad and make a wrap."

"I don't have to eat," I say hesitantly. "I don't want to disrupt your schedule or routine."

Gabe catches my eye with a smirk, and the impish grin on his face is contagious. "It's just a piece of salmon, Firecracker. I'll survive."

"Okay," I whisper. "I grew up with athletes, Gabe. I know all about what you guys do. I know your life has already been thrown a massive curveball, and now you've got a nanny living in your space and disrupting your life. I want to make this as easy of a transition for you as possible."

"Thank you for calling Mackenzie a curveball, and not something awful like a kink or a bomb," he murmurs.

"Oh, I'd never say that. She's so perfect, even when she's crabby for no reason."

"She really is," he says with a peaceful smile. "I always thought I'd have kids at some point, but didn't know when. I'm certainly not happy about her mom dying, but I will never regret getting to have Mackenzie in my life."

"I love that," I whisper, a smile tugging at my lips. He's going to be such an extraordinary dad.

"So obviously I know about Grant. What do the rest of your brothers do? He really only ever talks about you," Gabe says as he mixes the salads. Placing one in front of me at the table, he grabs two bottles of water and settles in across from me. I take a big bite of the salmon, the flavors bursting on my tongue as the salmon falls apart in tender chunks.

"This is really good," I comment, and Gabe grunts in agreement. "Grant's always been my best friend. I love my other brothers, but none of them see me like Grant does. He's always been my most faithful supporter, even when he doesn't fully agree with my choices."

"I think he's probably the brother that would absolutely help you bury a body."

"Probably," I respond, laughing. "He'd help, but then read me the riot act afterward."

"And then still lie to the police about it all."

"Of course! He'd protect me, but also not want to go to jail himself for being an accomplice."

"That does sound like Grant," Gabe chuckles. "And you have two other brothers?"

"Yeah. Tristan is thirty-five. He's the oldest, and he just retired from the NFL."

"Tristan McNally. I don't think I ever put it together that he's the NFL brother Grant talks about."

"He's pretty quiet. Doesn't hit the news very often. He just does his job and goes home."

"He's one of the best centers in the league, Cass. He's not just 'doing his job,'" Grant says, using air quotes. Smiling, he continues. "Grant would talk about his brother, but rarely use his name. It didn't occur to me. I rarely use your full last name. So it's possible I was associating Nally instead of McNally."

I shrug. "Tristan's pretty humble. He's not a fan of the media, so he rarely goes out of his way for interviews or public appearances. He prefers to give his time and money quietly. He even started a non-profit under an alias so that it can't become a media frenzy."

"Oh yeah? What's the non-profit for?"

"He's a big animal lover, so it benefits the greater Dallas area and all of their animal rescue organizations. Providing food, transportation, medical supplies."

"That's pretty cool. And your other brother?"

"Dylan plays for FC Portland."

"Ahh, a soccer player. Your parents really raised three kids in three different sports?" Gabe asks.

"Life was chaotic. I think our mom was thrilled when Tristan got his driver's license, because it meant she could hand over some of the carpooling responsibilities to him."

"That makes sense," Gabe says with a laugh. "And your parents still live in the Pacific Northwest?"

I nod. "They like having one of us there, but they enjoy traveling, so visiting everyone else isn't an issue. Do you have any siblings?"

"I have a sister. She's a teacher. She'll be the first to tell you that I got all of the athletic genes in our family. She lives in Pittsburgh."

"Is that where you're from? I can't remember if you've told me this."

"No, I'm from southeastern Ohio. My sister is a couple of hours from my parents."

"Was she into sports?" I ask.

"No," he says, laughing. "She's the brainiac of the family. I'm by no means stupid, but she's so damn smart."

"What does she teach?"

"High school calculus, algebra, and even teaches a couple of courses at a community college." Gabe's grin is massive as he brags about his sister. I'm loving this side of him.

"Sounds like she's a math whiz," I comment.

"She is. She certainly helped me in high school more times than I can count. Calculus is not my thing," he confesses.

I snort. "Mine either."

Gabe clears his throat as he stands to take our empty plates to the sink. As he busies himself with loading the dishwasher, he says, "Are you settling in okay? Do you need anything?"

"I'm settling in fine," I tell him, but the drastic switch in our conversation has me on high alert. "Is there something you're concerned about?"

"Well, not exactly," he stammers as he turns to face me. "I realize we didn't set some ground rules for, uh, extracurricular activities."

Confused, I say, "I don't think I plan on joining any sports leagues anytime soon."

"That's not what I meant," he mutters, scratching his head. "I'm just going to come out and say it. While you're under my roof, I'd appreciate it if you didn't bring any gentlemen back here."

My mouth drops open in astonishment. "Are you being for real right now?"

Gabe nods. "I have to take Mackenzie's safety and security into account."

"And you think I'd just bring some random guy into your home?"

"I don't know. You invited me back to your hotel room pretty quickly," he points out.

"A hotel room is nowhere near the same thing, and you know it," I snap. "Turnabout is fair play. Will you be abiding by the same rule?"

"I have no intention of bringing any women home. But, this is *my* house. Rules for me can be different from rules for you."

"Why?" I ask, crossing my arms in anger. This is bullshit. Do as I say, not as I do. "Women can be just as dangerous as men."

"I'm not bringing a one-night stand home. I've never done that, and I don't intend to start now. However, if I were to start seriously dating someone, the rule doesn't apply to me."

"Well, if that's the case, then I'd like a warning."

"A warning for what?"

"If you're dating someone. If she'll be at the house. Where that leaves me."

Gabe's lips thin as his eyes narrow. "What the fuck does that mean?"

"If you have a serious girlfriend, you might not need a nanny anymore. I'd like to be notified so I have adequate time to look for a new job, Gabe."

"Oh," he says, rubbing the bridge of his nose. "I thought you meant ... you know what? Never mind."

"No, go ahead," I challenge him. "Tell me what you thought."

He sighs, looking up at the ceiling. "I thought you meant where that left us. You and me. Because we've slept together, and I thought maybe you thought this was going somewhere. Which it's not."

Well, that hurts. I wasn't thinking about that, but it still sucks hearing it from him. "You made that clear when you hired me, Gabe. I have no hopes or aspirations of something happening between us."

"Good," he states. "But to circle back, I don't have any intention of bringing someone home. If anything changes with my relationship status, I'll let you know."

"Likewise."

"Huh?" he asks, a bewildered expression covering his gorgeous face.

"If my relationship status changes, I'll let *you* know."

"I just said I don't want you bringing someone into my house, Cassie," he says angrily.

I wave a hand nonchalantly at him, effectively shushing him. How dare he suggest I'm not allowed to date at all! I'm shutting this battle down right fucking now. "I said I wouldn't bring anyone here. I never said I wouldn't go to their houses. I'm a single woman, and I have ... needs, Gabe."

The look he gives me is downright feral, and sheer lust flows over me. "I know exactly what your needs are, Firecracker. And I'm willing to bet you won't be able to find anyone who meets your needs better than me."

He's totally right, but I'm not letting him know that. "Eh. I'm not sure you're *that* special, Gabe. You do at least know where the clit is, I'll give you that."

He growls, and I feel it in my core. "That's how you want to play this? You and I both know that —"

A sharp cry fills the air, forcing us to stop talking. With a huff,

Gabe strides past me, and I let out a relieved exhale I didn't know I was holding.

Cassie

CHAPTER 5

The following week, Gabe and I took shifts with Mackenzie. He was a healthy scratch for the team, courtesy of his coaches, allowing us to develop a routine with each other. I was always available, should he need extra help, but he never asked for anything. It shouldn't surprise me that Gabe turned out to be an excellent father. He's very hands-on, and his love for Mackenzie oozes from his pores. It makes him even more attractive. Dammit.

The night before he's ready to join the team again, I can tell he's nervous about leaving Mackenzie. Besides taking a nap, showering, or running a quick errand, he hasn't been apart from her since they left the hospital. Tonight, his mood is different. It's agitated. Nervous. Borderline chaotic. As he gives Mackenzie her evening bottle, his leg jiggles constantly. Without thinking, I grab his knee to stop his leg from moving. When his eyes dart to mine, I see the confusion in his gaze.

"Crap, sorry," I mutter. "Stop shaking your leg. You might make her spit up."

"Dammit," he spits out. "I just ... I don't want to leave."

"I know," I say softly.

His gaze is intense as he stares at me. "It's not about you. You know that, right? I'm not apprehensive about you keeping her. I know she's in good hands. But —"

"But they aren't your hands. I get it, Gabe. Really, I do."

"I've never hated hockey before. This is new," he chuckles bitterly.

"It's okay to be sad. She's your baby. You can hate being away from her, and fearful of not being in control."

"Millions of people leave their children for work every day. I feel like I'm making too big of a deal about this." Gabe runs his hands through his hair quickly, the motion unsettling his wavy locks. His jaw clenches as he grabs the back of his neck in frustration.

"I don't think so," I tell him. "You're in a unique situation. It isn't just a nine-to-five job. And most people don't leave town right away. You didn't have any time to plan for this either, Gabe. You're well within your rights to be freaked out about everything."

"I'm lucky the team let me have two weeks off," he says absent-mindedly.

"That isn't standard paternity leave?" I ask.

He shakes his head. "Hockey comes first. They might give a couple days, but getting two weeks off is pretty atypical, especially leading up to the playoffs."

"Unique set of circumstances."

"I guess," he murmurs, his brow furrowed as he stares at Mackenzie. "Are you going to be okay? I'll be gone tomorrow morning, then again tomorrow evening. I'll come home and take a nap in the afternoon."

"Pre-game nap," I chuckle, and Gabe smiles in understanding.

"Yep. Grant has a whole series of stupid superstitions he does throughout a game day, but for me, it's always been about the nap, and about the socks I wear."

"I bet you put them on in a specific order, though," I tease him, and he laughs.

"I do."

I shake my head in mock disappointment. "You damn hockey boys and your superstitions."

"I'd take offense, but you're not wrong. Actually, the guys teased me because they said I needed a new tradition after I got a hat trick a few weeks ago —" Gabe abruptly stops talking.

"You got a hat trick? That's amazing!" I gush. A hat trick is when one player scores three goals in the same game. "So what do they want you to do now?"

"Nothing, it's nothing," he says hurriedly. "You saved all the numbers I sent you, right?"

The quick change of topic is like whiplash, but I don't ask what is going on. "Yes, I have every single number for the team, all the coaches, the front office at the practice arena and the main arena, and a bunch of other employees. Who is Elsie, by the way? She texted me today and told me she was on standby if I needed you."

"Physical therapist for the team, and the coach's girlfriend," Gabe answers as he stands up. "I'm going to give baby girl a bath, then get her settled in for the night. Are you okay with taking the night shift tonight?"

"Of course," I answer, again put off by his quick response and tone. I cock my head to the side, studying him, and I realize he won't make eye contact with me. "What happened a couple weeks ago that made you get a hat trick, Gabe?"

He sighs, closes his eyes, and then says, "I met you."

Stunned, I can't find words to respond as I watch him walk upstairs.

"Cass," I hear whispered.
"Hmm?"
"Cassie."

"Huh?"

"Cassie, Mackenzie is awake, and I need to leave for practice."

I bolt upright as I realize Gabe is actually talking to me. In my dream, he was very much not doing any talking, but his lips were definitely moving. Rubbing my eyes, I stare up at Gabe. Hovering above me, he's in workout clothes and holding a to-go cup of coffee. When my eyes meet his, I see they are bloodshot and weary. "Did you not get any sleep last night?"

"No."

"Nervous about today?" I ask.

"No. Mackenzie was up all night." His answer is blunt, and do I hear a slight accusatory tone?

"Gabe! I said I'd take her!" I whisper-yell as I throw the comforter off his guest bed and stand up.

"*That's* why. That's why you didn't take her," Gabe growls, his tone accusatory as he points at my body. I look down and realize I'm in a tank top and a thong. "I came in here to hand her off, and you were sprawled half under the blankets, and your ass was on display, and I couldn't wake you up at that point, now could I?"

"You absolutely could have woken me up because that's what you're paying me to do! This is how I sleep, Gabe, so you better get used to it!"

"You can put fucking pants on to sleep, god dammit," he growls.

"You walk around half-naked all the time, and you're gonna tell me how to dress when I'm sleeping? That's rich," I retort.

"I do not walk around half-naked!"

"Yeah, you totally do. And don't you dare tell me it's for skin-to-skin. That was cool the first night, but now it's just you hoping I'll stare." I stare. I try not to, but I can't help it. He's like a car crash. I want to look away, but I can't.

"Clearly, you do, or you wouldn't notice I'm walking around half-naked." Gabe's breathing has picked up, his chest expanding quicker and quicker as he stands over me.

"So you do admit it! Do you need a confidence boost, Mr. Big

Time Hockey Man?" Have we gotten closer together? What the hell is happening right now?

"God dammit!" he yells before yanking me toward him and covering my lips with his. Gabe turns and pushes me against the wall, his hands finding my ass and lifting me. My legs automatically wrap around his waist as his tongue forces its way into my mouth. He groans into me as I slide my hands up into his hair, my nails scratching harshly along his neck and scalp. I probably have ridiculous morning breath, but he doesn't seem to mind.

As Gabe's hand begins to slide toward my center, a piercing cry breaks through my hazy mind, and I become cognizant of what just happened. Breaking off the kiss, I dislodge my legs and drop to the ground, pushing him away from me. I reach up and touch my lips, swollen and hot from his kiss, and I wonder if they look like Gabe's. His gaze is hazy as he roughly runs one hand through his hair.

"I need to leave," he grits out.

"Okay," I stammer, then rush past him into his room to collect Mackenzie. I hear Gabe stomp down the stairs before opening and slamming the front door. Going to the window, I see him stand in the driveway for a moment, his hands clenched tightly into fists before he walks back to the door. I giggle quietly as I hear him shuffle through the house and out into the garage. Looking down at Mackenzie, I notice she's staring intently at me. "Your daddy is kinda nuts."

When she coos at me, I decide she agrees.

The morning goes remarkably well. Since it's my first time fully alone in the house with Mackenzie, I somehow expected she would have difficulty with the transition. I'm pretty sure a three-week-old baby is mostly only aware of eating, sleeping, and pooping. After a rousing tummy time resulted in some impressive explosive vomiting, I gave Mackenzie a bath. Then, I set her down for her late morning nap. When she kept fussing and couldn't seem to get fully settled, I pulled the bassinet up against Gabe's' bed and decided to rest my head until she settled. Surrounded by the aroma of Gabe's cologne, I relaxed and fell asleep.

When I wake up, I know something is different. I'm hot. And I feel like my body is heavy. Opening one eye, I find Mackenzie still peacefully sleeping, so I decide to quietly leave the room to do some laundry. But I can't seem to get up.

I hear a sigh behind me, and an arm tightens around my midsection. It's then that I realize Gabe is wrapped around me. I must stiffen because Gabe murmurs, "Just sleep, Cass. Don't overthink it. I need this."

He needs what exactly? Sleep? Me? A body, *any* body, to hold onto? Thankfully, Mackenzie stirs, and I have an excuse to get up. "Let me take Kenzie out so you can rest."

Gabe sighs again and reluctantly removes his arm from around my waist.

Grabbing Kenzie, I nuzzle against her cheek and whisper, "Let's give Daddy space for his nap time, pretty girl."

"Like that," Gabe mutters.

"What?"

"You calling her pretty girl. And you calling me Daddy."

Oh.

I stumble out of his bedroom without a response.

Mackenzie and I settle into a pattern of sorts. Now that Gabe is fully back with the team, I can relax into caring for her, and ignoring the growing tension between Gabe and me. We've never spoken about the kiss, or the spooning during a nap, but every time I'm in a room with Gabe, I feel a heat forcefully pressing down on me. It's oppressive with how it tries to push me toward him.

The night before Gabe is scheduled to leave for his last extended road trip of the regular season, it all comes to a head. Gabe is packing his suitcase in the living room as Mackenzie is asleep in her bassinet in his room. The monitor on the end table gives us a bird's-eye view of the bassinet, and Gabe looks at it every couple of minutes.

"I expect hourly updates, and at least two FaceTimes per day, Cassie."

"I already told you I'd do all of that," I say warily. Gabe is so keyed up that I'm ready for him to leave so he can get over this major hurdle.

"You understand it's not that I will be checking up on your ability to care for my daughter?"

"Yes, Gabe."

He sighs angrily as he slams a handful of shirts into his suitcase. "I don't think I'll be able to concentrate unless I know she's okay."

"I know."

He looks up at me, his eyes a storm of emotions. "She became my whole world in one short month."

"I know, Gabe. I'll update you as often as possible, and send you lots of pictures."

"Just don't send anything the hour before the puck drops. It might throw me off."

For fuck's sake. "Then turn off your damn phone. You'll be gallivanting around the country, through multiple time zones, and I'm not gonna do math to try and figure out if it's within an hour of your game or not."

"It's not that hard. Just look up the start time and find the time zone," Gabe mutters, his eyes narrowing. His lips might be pursed in annoyance, but his eyes keep darting to look at my mouth. Oh yes.

"I'm not doing that. Turn off your damn phone," I repeat.

His gaze snaps to mine as his jaw clenches in anger. But those eyes, the beautiful brown eyes that currently seem to be undressing me slowly, smolder. "You'll do whatever I tell you to do because I'm fucking paying you to do it."

"No."

"Yes." He approaches me, his stance taut with both power and sensuality.

"Oh yeah? How are you gonna make me?" I taunt, knowing exactly what's about to happen. I'm poking the bear, and I fully intend to reap the benefits.

"Motherfucker," Gabe swears as he grabs me and crushes our lips together. The moment we connect, my soul sings in bliss. I think I needed this. Needed him. I need him like I've never experienced before. The tension between us slowly built until we combusted.

Our tongues duel in harmony as we both grab hungrily at each other, my hands scratching up and down his back while his latch into my hair and maneuver my head in whatever direction he wants. Gabe is hot. Daddy Gabe is fire. But dominant Gabe? Take charge Gabe? Holy shit, it's an inferno.

Gabe picks me up and walks to the kitchen, depositing me on the bar. It's higher than the counters, and I'm unsure of his intentions. "What are you doing?"

He pulls up a chair and sits down, a feral grin covering his face, and I find my core is at the perfect height for his mouth. "Eating. Take off your fucking pants."

When I don't move fast enough, he grabs hold of the waistband of my leggings and yanks them off, taking my panties with them, and slides both hands up my legs seductively until his hands rest on my inner thighs. When I tremble with need, he smiles. "That's my girl. Tell me what you want, Cassie."

Jesus, I could come just from his voice. Somehow, it's deeper, raspier, and downright carnal how he's speaking to me.

"Use your words, Firecracker," Gabe coaxes as one finger skirts along the seam of my pussy, but not enough to touch anything.

"I — I want to come," I stammer.

"I know that, baby. How do you want to come? With my mouth? Fingers? My cock? Do you want it rough, or do you want me to edge you for hours?"

"You have to sleep," I whimper. "You need to be rested for your trip."

"No, I need this. I need you. Now fucking tell me how you'll let me have you," Gabe murmurs, his voice like honey being poured on my skin.

"All of it, I want all of it! Make me come with your tongue, Gabe. Please!" I cry out. I attempt to slide my fingers down and take the edge off by touching my clit, but he slaps my hand away. Gabe slides one finger inside my channel, and my body automatically clamps down on him. He finds my G-spot and rubs, ever so slowly, but backs off as soon as he recognizes I'm about to come. Needing some relief, I grab my breasts, pinching my nipples harshly, but Gabe pulls one arm down.

"I'll get you off, Cass. *I'll* do it. Don't you dare try to take *my* orgasm from me."

Holy shit. The mouth on this man.

"Then do it, god dammit!" I shout, ready to shove him away and take care of it myself. I'm so turned on I'm shaking. I think we've been edging each other for the last two weeks. Like a pot of water, slowly heating up, building until a rolling boil threatens to spill over. God, I need this. I ache with need for him.

I again slide my fingers down, needing anything on my clit to give me a little release of the pressure building inside me, and Gabe slaps my hand away again. Two fingers slide inside this time, and thankfully, he applies more pressure to my G-spot. "Come on, hurry, please!"

I open my eyes to look at Gabe, and find a thunderous expression covering his gorgeous face. I expect another verbal tongue-lashing, but what I get instead is an *actual* tongue-lashing. His head disappears between my legs, and I finally feel the velvety softness of his tongue against my clit. It doesn't take much, though. A quick flick, flick, flick, and I combust. My back bows off the counter as a fierce orgasm overtakes me, my entire body shaking as pleasure courses throughout my veins. But Gabe doesn't stop. He builds me right back up, sending me over again and again until I push his head away. Still shuddering, my vagina has a damn pulse, and he's looking at me like he could sit here all night, feasting on my pussy.

"I can't," I whimper.

"You can't what?" He straightens his back, and I peer at him. His scruff is wet, evidence of my multiple orgasms. Gabe's pupils are blown so wide I can't tell where they stop and his irises begin. He's panting as hard as I am, almost as if he got off on getting me off.

"Too sensitive," I finally answer.

I feel one finger slowly slide into my channel, immediately finding my G-spot, and I let out a guttural moan. "Oh, I think you've got at least a few more in there, baby."

A second finger joins in, and then Gabe takes his other hand and presses it against my lower abdomen. The pressure is unlike anything I've ever experienced. I feel like I need to pee, but a spark ignites in my core. I'm thrashing on the counter as I both push toward Gabe and also away from him, confused by what I'm feeling. I've never felt an intensity like this. It's overtaking my entire body, and when Gabe leans forward to latch onto my clit, nibbling it softly, I shatter. I feel a gush as Gabe pushes his hands together like he's trying to get them to meet inside me, and an orgasm like I've never felt before rumbles through my system. I let out a long moan as I ride the wave of the best high I've ever gotten.

Gabe carefully slides his arms underneath me, picks me up, and carries me to the couch. He goes to lay me down, but I throw my legs down and then push him onto the couch.

"You need to rest, Firecracker," he says, but I shake my head.

"No. I need to feel you. You said you needed me a few weeks ago. During your nap, remember? Well, now I'm telling you that I need this. I need it so badly, Gabe. Please," I whisper. He pushes an errant hair behind my ears and gives me a soft smile.

"Are you worried about blurring the lines?" he asks.

I hesitate, wondering if I should be honest, or feed him a line about this being just one time. To scratch an itch. To get rid of this stifling energy that hovers over us whenever we're together. Anything. But what comes out is, "The lines were blurred the moment I stepped into your bedroom that first night."

Gabe

CHAPTER 6

She's right. The lines are blurred. Hell, there aren't any lines. I've been creeping around her for days, trying to *will* my dick to behave. Being in close proximity to her has been torture. I forgot how responsive she is. Our chemistry is exceptional, and I know in my soul that I don't want this to be the only time for this. But I'm afraid to say anything.

"Let's take it one step at a time," Cassie says shyly.

I nod in agreement. That's better than a firm no, so I'll take it.

Her lips meet mine in a soft kiss. It's tender, so different from anything we've experienced so far. I let her take control, and I feel her tongue tentatively touch the seam of my lips before slowly sliding in to touch mine. She whimpers into my mouth, and I wonder if she's tasting herself. She shifts, almost imperceptibly, and the heat from her bare and sopping wet pussy soaks through my joggers, making my cock like fucking steel.

Breaking off the kiss, I pat her ass. "Can you go grab my wallet? Think I've got a condom in there."

Cassie quickly jumps up, and I have an insane vision of her in nothing but my jersey as I watch her prance over to the table where my wallet is. The thought of coming home one night and finding her in just my jersey, begging me to fuck her ... damn.

I immediately peel down my joggers and kick them off as she walks back to me. Cassie straddles my lap, circling right above the tip, and gasps when it hits her clit perfectly. "Put the condom on, baby."

Cassie's hands shake ever so slightly as she rips open the package and gently slides the condom down my length. Just the slight touch of her fingers has me hissing in pleasure and need. I can't remember the last time I was this anxious to fuck someone. I feel like my body is so tense that the moment she sinks down on me, I won't be able to keep from rutting into her. I think I might lose control in her.

"Gabe," she whispers. Our eyes meet, and her gaze is heavy. A beautiful flush covers Cassie's cheeks and neck, and I'm desperate to see if it trails down to her tits. I pull her shirt off as she slowly positions me, then slams herself down.

"Fuuuuck," I groan as I lean forward and bite her nipple through her bra. My hands find her hips to encourage her to move faster. Her cries of pleasure reverberate around the room, and I grab her head to bring it to mine. "Don't wake Mackenzie."

"Oh, God, I'm so sorry," she says, a stricken expression covering her face.

"Don't apologize. Kiss me. Any sound you make, I'll swallow it. Be as loud as you want, baby. Don't hold back," I tell her, crashing our lips together as I quicken the pace again. Cassie doesn't stay quiet. Her mewls and cries are like a balm to my soul; her nails digging into my shoulders are reaching in to grab hold of my heart. The closer we both get to orgasm, the more attached we become. I can't see where she ends, and I begin. Cassie buries her head in my neck, her hair blanketing my body.

"I'm almost there," she whispers in my ear, and I'm relieved to hear it because I'm two seconds from blowing without her. Reaching around, I press my forefinger against her tight rosebud, and that's all it takes for Cassie to stiffen in my arms. She throws her head back and whispers my name as she comes. It's one of the most beautiful things I've ever had the pleasure of experiencing, and it sets off my own explosive orgasm. Cassie collapses against me as we both try to catch our breath.

Damn. It's not how I saw the night going, but I'm not complaining.

"That was ..." Cassie trails off.

"Intense," I finish.

"Yeah."

"Are you okay?" we both ask simultaneously, then laugh together.

"I'm great," she says with a light giggle. "Can't complain."

"I meant with this happening at all. You were saying you didn't want to blur the lines."

"I also meant what I said when I told you the lines were blurred ages ago." Cassie gingerly slides off of me, wincing as she collapses beside me on the couch. "I forgot how big you are. I'm gonna be feeling this tomorrow."

"I'd apologize, but I'm not even a little bit sorry," I tell her cheerfully.

She laughs as she stretches her legs out. "Clearly."

I let a moment of silence pass before clearing my throat. "But we're good? I don't want to leave tomorrow with things left unsaid."

Cassie sighs. "I'm not sure what I want to say just yet. I think I need some time to process what just happened."

"Oh," I say, the wind knocked out of my sails. "Okay."

"Guess it's good you'll be gone for ten days, huh," she jokes, but I don't laugh. I debate on telling her that tonight was eye-opening for me. How it affirmed what I've been feeling since I met her, and that I want more. But before I can, Cassie stands up, retrieves her pants and underwear, and turns to me. "If Mackenzie is asleep when you leave in the morning, just bring me the monitor. She's been sleeping in a little later every morning this week."

I nod weakly as she walks to the stairs, feeling worse and worse with each step she takes away from me. At the bottom of the staircase, she turns. "Good luck this week, Gabe. Don't worry about us. We'll be fine here, and I promise to send you tons of updates."

Cassie gives me a smile before she quietly heads upstairs. I hear her enter her room, and I'm taken aback by how quickly the night turned. I let out an aggravated breath as I grab my hair and pull hard. Standing, I pull up my pants and walk to the bathroom to deal with the condom.

When both Mackenzie and Cassie are sound asleep the following morning, I sneak into Cassie's room and leave her the baby monitor. Standing above her, I want to shake her awake and tell her she needs to get on board with ... something. Hell, even I don't know what to call this thing with her. The fact that I'm paying her to nanny my daughter complicates things. If I asked her to date me, would that be some gray area? Could it be viewed as prostitution? I wouldn't think of it that way, but would she?

Those thoughts make me doubt whether Cassie and I can move forward with anything, so I don't wake her up. Instead, I lean down and press a soft kiss to her temple. She sighs my name before rolling over, and I quickly leave the room before she wakes up. Heading back into my room, I quietly peer into Mackenzie's crib. I can feel tears building behind my eyes as I stare at her. I fucking hate having to leave her. I don't know how other guys on the team do it.

An hour later, I'm on the team plane, flipping through the hundreds of pictures of my daughter on my camera roll.

"You're gonna be miserable all week, aren't you?" Jax says as he drops heavily into the seat beside me. I look over to see Levi wearing a smirk as he waits for my reply.

"Yeah, he's gonna be miserable," Grant adds as he throws a bag onto the seat in front of me. He ducks his head over to look at my phone and dramatically sighs. "Jesus. How many pictures do you have of her already?"

"Not nearly enough," I retort.

"I liked the one you sent where she looked stoned out of her mind," Jax comments.

"It's called being milk drunk. Let's not refer to my child as being stoned," I reply drolly.

Levi looks at his phone and appears to be counting. "You've sent us twenty-five pictures in the group text. I'm a little disappointed, Daws. Thought for sure you'd be in triple digits by now. Grant's sister will probably send you twenty pics a day."

She damn well better. But the thought of Cassie makes me feel awkward. She rocked my world hours ago, and now her brother is staring at me. And now he's glaring.

"God dammit!" he shouts. "You fucked her again, didn't you? What the hell, Gabe? I thought she'd be safe there because of Mackenzie!"

"Lower your fucking voice!" I hiss.

Grant growls at me. "Tell me I'm wrong. You better not be taking advantage of my sister."

"I'm not taking advantage of her," I say defensively. "That would insinuate we both weren't on the same page. We're adults, Grant. There were no advantages in this situation."

"I still don't understand how you met her weeks ago, man. What are the chances?" he asks, his gaze still calculating as he studies me.

I sigh in frustration. "I swear there were no ulterior motives. I'm not sure you mentioned Cassie moving here, and I certainly didn't scope out where she might stay. The city is pretty big, man. Never thought I'd run into her at one of my favorite hole-in-the-wall restaurants. I wanted to ask for her number, Nally. You have to believe me. I had every intention of seeing her again."

"Sounds like it was kismet. Karma or something. Meant to be," Levi comments before turning his phone around and showing me a photo I've never seen of Mackenzie.

"Where did you get that one?" I ask.

"Cassie sent it to me," he says casually.

"What?" I growl.

"We exchanged numbers that first night after you stomped upstairs. I asked for some Kenzie pics, and she's been sending them regularly."

"Are you fucking serious? Are you hitting on my nanny?" I awkwardly stand, my height not allowing me to fully extend. I attempt to jump over Jax and get in Levi's face, but Jax and Grant stop me.

"Dude, no. I just asked for some pics of your kid. Nothing else. You made it clear from the moment you saw Cassie that she was yours," Levi says, hands up in mock surrender. Jax puts a hand on my shoulder to shove me back into my seat.

"I made it clear?" I ask.

"Fuck yeah, you did," Jax chortles. When I catch his eyes, he shrugs. "You gave off a vibe, Daws. If you could have peed on her to mark her as yours, you would have."

"I didn't want anything to happen," I admit. "But I've felt this pull to Cassie since the first moment I saw her, and it's only gotten stronger since she moved in."

"What are you going to do about it?" Levi asks quietly.

"Nothing, I guess."

"Why?" Grant shouts. When I look at him in surprise, his intensity gives me pause. "You talked about that girl for a good week after you met. Had I known it was my sister, I would have stopped some of the conversations, but still. You clearly connected with her, and then for her to be my sister and in need of a job? I agree with Levi. I think you two are meant to be."

"Weren't you just pissed that I slept with her again?" I ask warily.

Grant shrugs, his expression nonplussed. "I certainly don't want to hear any details since I know it's my sister, but it's pretty damn clear you're both into one another. Sure, it was a shock when I realized you'd hooked up with her, but she's an adult. I can't treat her like a baby, even though I want to. You treat women with respect, and there are worse assholes out there she could be with. Frankly, you're one of the nicest guys on the team, and you rarely cause problems. Except for when you tried to hook up with Luca's girl."

"I heard that," Luca shouts from a few rows back.

"I didn't really try to hook up with Hannah --" I stop as all three guys look at me in shock. "Okay, so maybe I wasn't opposed to something happening with her, but I stepped aside as soon as I realized she was into Santzy. I'm not into that kind of bullshit on the team."

"Remember when you told us you just wanted to hit it and quit it, right outside her office door?" Levi asks.

I feel a slight heat cover my face. "That may have not been the most eloquent thing to do. I knew Luca was in there, though, and it seemed like a good time to fuck with him. But other than that, I really don't want to deal with a toxic situation."

"Exactly," Grant agrees. "You're genuine, except, apparently, when you get to fuck with Santzy, and I know you'd treat Cassie right. If you want to pursue her, I won't stand in your way."

"Go for it, man. I think you'd be great together," Jax says seriously, and Levi nods in agreement.

"There's a big problem here, gentlemen. You're leaving one variable out of this equation," I say with a bitter chuckle.

"What?" Jax asks.

"Cassie."

"So?" Levi says. "And?"

"I don't think she wants anything with me." Sucks even saying that out loud. But the vibe she gave off last night was ... cold. Colder than I anticipated. And I'm afraid to ask her what the deal is.

"What do you mean?" Grant asks.

I look up at him exasperatedly. "Can we not talk about this? It's your sister."

"Just explain a little bit. Without any specific details involving either of your bodies or sounds you make or —" Grant breaks off with an exaggerated gag. All the guys laugh, even me.

"It's a vibe I got. She feels it would blur the lines, and she's afraid of pushing too far."

"And what do you want, Daws?" Jax asks.

"I'd like to see where things could go with her. I could see being happy with Cassie."

Levi gasps dramatically. "Our boy is growing up!"

"Aw!" Jax coos and Grant smacks him on the back of the head.

"Alright Dawsy, I'm not gonna butt my nose in and screw with things. But I will say this: I know my sister. And you're right. She's probably in her head about things. If you're meant to be, it'll happen. Right now, your focus for the next ten days is hockey. Let Cassie work through things independently, and let her care for your daughter. Although I gotta admit, I'd be cool if Kenzie ended up being my niece at some point," Grant says with a wink before he turns around and sits in his seat.

"What should I do in the meantime? When I have to interact with Cassie?" I wonder aloud.

"Do what you've normally done. You've spoken to Cassie every day since she moved in, right? No difference now. Ask how she's doing, then move the convo to talk about Mackenzie. Be nice and cordial, but don't ask about whatever happened between you." Jax leans toward me and whispers, "It was good, though, right? Did you enjoy it as much as the first time?"

"More," I blurt out.

Grant swears in front of us. "I fucking told you to leave out the details!"

"He really needs to get laid," Jax mutters.

"I heard that," Grant snaps.

Cassie

CHAPTER 7

I faked being asleep the morning he left. I got spooked and ran after our amazing sex, and I couldn't look him in the eye that morning. I did, however, take a peek at the baby monitor screen sitting beside my bed, and watched him struggle to walk away from Mackenzie. It made me fall a little more for him, which scares the shit out of me.

The first few days of Gabe's long road trip are beyond awkward. Neither one of us knows how to talk to the other. Our text conversations are random details about stupid stuff until we begin discussing Mackenzie. Then, the convo flows nicely.

ME
It's sunny today.

GABE
Rain here.

ME
Where are you?

GABE
Seattle

ME

Did you go to the Space Needle? Or Pike Place?

GABE

No to the first one, and I don't know what the second one is.

ME

It's the famous fish market where they throw the fish.

GABE

Oh.

ME

You got a box in the mail.

GABE

New shoes, I think.

ME

Want me to open and check?

GABE

No.

GABE

Just new sneakers. Red ones.

ME

Why red?

GABE

Favorite color.

ME

I hope it's alright, but I've been sleeping in your room. It's been easier to grab Kenzie when she wakes up at night.

ME

I got this book about sleep regressions, and I think she's going through one. She's been waking up four or five extra times a night.

ME

Since you didn't answer me, I figured it upset you, so I moved her crib into my room.

GABE

Okay.

GABE

Can you send me a couple of pictures of Kenz, please? My mom wants some updated ones.

ME

Sure. Would you like to send them directly to her? I know you're super busy and focused on hockey. I'm happy to coordinate the exchange. I can get some printed and send them to her if you'd like.

GABE

Not necessary. I'll handle it.

GABE

How's my girl doing?

ME

I'm doing well, thanks for asking.

GABE

Uh, I meant my daughter.

ME

Oh. Kenzie's fine. Lasted for twenty minutes doing tummy time this morning.

GABE

That's the longest she's lasted, right?

ME

Yeah. She's not a fan of it.

GABE

What's the point of tummy time?

ME

Strengthening neck muscles and making sure she doesn't have a flat head. The bones in her skull are still developing and fusing together. If she spends too much time on her back, her skull bones will fuse together in a different position than what is ideal.

GABE

Wow. I had no idea. The baby book I'm reading hasn't covered tummy time yet.

> **ME**
> You're reading a baby book?
>
> **GABE**
> Yeah. I put the Kindle app on my phone and found some books I can read there.
>
> **ME**
> That's actually really cool. My Kindle doesn't have many nonfiction books.

Honestly, I don't think there's one nonfiction book on my Kindle. I like what I like, and I don't deviate from it. The world is a dumpster fire most of the time, so it's nice to escape into a romance book when I need a pick-me-up.

> **GABE**
> What are you currently reading?
>
> **ME**
> A fictional story about a sports professional who finds a baby dropped on his doorstep and navigates new fatherhood while simultaneously engaging in a romantic relationship with his best friend's daughter.
>
> **GABE**
> So you're reading porn?
>
> **ME**
> IT IS NOT PORN.
>
> **ME**
> Well, it kinda is.
>
> **GABE**
> Title, please.
>
> **ME**
> No.

GABE

Come on. We have a five-hour flight tomorrow. I can only read so much about babies. Porn will be a nice change.

ME

Are you going to judge me about the content?

GABE

No.

ME

...

GABE

Maybe a little.

ME

...

GABE

It might teach me some things.

ME

Lovely.

GABE

Just give me the title.

ME

A Major Puck Up by Brittanée Nicole.

GABE

It's porn.

ME

It is NOT.

GABE

Alright, it's borderline porn. Is this what women like to read? About grown men fucking teenagers?

ME

She's twenty-two in the book, Gabe.

GABE

Fine. Fucking ALMOST teenagers.

ME

Ew. No. Well, I guess some women probably do like to read that stuff. I'm not about to yuck someone's yum.

GABE

Yuck someone's yum? That's new.

ME

It's like making fun of someone and telling them they're wrong for liking a specific sports team. We're all allowed to like what we like.

GABE

Within reason.

ME

Yes.

GABE

You're not into some weird shit, are you? Like reading about people getting fucked by horses, or a tentacled man drilling all your holes at the same time?

ME

Boy. You did some weird Googling, didn't you?

GABE

I did.

ME

> No, I'm not into that kind of stuff. I like regular romance, where the guy sweeps her off her feet, and they feel like their connection is special. Like they weren't fully complete until that other person came into their lives.

I'm a little nervous when Gabe doesn't respond for quite some time after my last text. I don't know if it got too close to his game time, if he fell asleep, or if he chose not to respond, and I'm frankly too much of a chicken-shit to blatantly ask him why he didn't reply.

What worries me, however, is that I'm not entirely sure if I'm scared Gabe might tell me sleeping together was a mistake because he doesn't feel a connection with me ... or if he'll tell me that he *did* feel something.

I know I may have freaked out immediately after and hightailed it up to my room to cower. It's possible that I realized I'm nowhere near the extroverted person that Gabe met in the hotel, and I'm worried he'll be less attracted to me when he realizes I'm one heck of an introvert. My idea of a fun Friday night is a trip to a bookstore and then reading by a fire. I'm not interested in clubs or parties. I'm very content in my own little bubble, thank you.

But whatever is happening — or happened — with Gabe suddenly makes me take stock of my life. I'm thirty years old. I left Oregon because I was working a job I hated for a large daycare in a massive corporation. I love working with kids, but my four-year early childhood education degree hasn't been highly sought after. Whenever I was offered a job, the pay would usually be close to minimum wage. The Pacific Northwest is absurdly expensive. All three of my brothers have often offered me loans, but I don't take handouts. I never have. Our parents taught us to make our own way. So, instead of asking anyone for money, I decided a complete life change was needed. Colorado has slightly cheaper housing and day-to-day expenses. As soon as Grant was traded here, I knew I wanted to follow him. The state calls to me.

Certainly didn't see life evolving the way it has since I moved here though.

When Gabe doesn't text me the following day, I get concerned. I found highlights of his game through Google, so I at least know he's alive. But then Levi texts me and asks how Kenzie is, and I get pissed.

> **LEVI**
> Any new pictures today?

> **ME**
> (see attachment)

> **LEVI**
> I swear she's grown since we left.

> **ME**
> I think so. She almost smiled at me today, too. But it might have just been gas.

> **LEVI**
> One of my sisters used to always do that. It's about time for Kenzie to start smiling, though. The average is one to two months.

> **ME**
> It's weird how much you know about babies.

> **LEVI**
> I'm the oldest of a gazillion siblings, and I helped my mom a lot. Plus, I just like kids.

> **LEVI**
> Has Kenz still been spitting up?

> **LEVI**
> How's tummy time going?

> **LEVI**
> Did you take her to her four-week well-child appointment? What did the pediatrician say?

Motherfucker.

> **ME**
> Levi.

> **LEVI**
> What?

> **ME**
> Tell Gabe if he wants to know these things, he can FUCKING TEXT OR CALL ME HIMSELF.

> **LEVI**
> Busted.

> **ME**
> Don't text me again.

> **LEVI**
> But I still like hearing about Mackenzie!

> **ME**
> Ask Gabe about her. I won't be used as a middlewoman.

Five minutes later, my phone rings.

"What?" I shout.

"You can't keep information about my daughter from me!" Gabe snaps, his voice tense and angry.

"You can't use your friend as a reconnaissance man to track down information about your daughter!" I volley. "What the hell is wrong with you? Why wouldn't you just text me?"

"Because our text conversations have been weird. And now I don't... fuck. Never mind."

"What? Gabe, please talk to me. I don't want this to be awkward between us, but you're being super sketchy right now."

The phone remains quiet for a few minutes. It's quiet for so long that I pull the phone away from my ear to check if the call has been disconnected.

"I don't know how to act around you now," he finally says.

"Now?"

"Yeah."

"Since we had sex?"

"No. Since you said you needed to process things."

Oh.

"I didn't need to process *that*," I say hastily. "I think I ran away because I was scared of what you might say, so I wanted to beat you to the punch."

"What did you think I might say?" Gabe asks quietly.

I hesitate, wondering if I should be truthful, before taking a deep breath and telling him what I'm thinking. "That you thought it was a mistake."

Gabe lets out a loud exhale. "Christ, Cassie. I'd never think you were a mistake."

My heart skips a beat at that statement. And, of course, as I'm about to ask Gabe what he wants for us, Mackenzie has an explosive diaper situation. "Crap, I gotta go. I also mean literal crap. Your daughter just shot poop out of the side of her onesie."

"I'm oddly proud of that," Gabe chuckles.

"Text me your questions from now on, okay? No more going through Levi."

"I will, Firecracker."

When the call ends, I realize he called me by the nickname he bestowed upon me the first night we met, making my insides feel gooey.

On the sixth day of the road trip, I'm lounging with Mackenzie on the living room carpet while she does tummy time, and the doorbell rings. Expecting it's another package for Gabe, I open it without looking through the peephole. Gabe lives in a really nice neighborhood. I probably should be more careful about things when caring for his daughter, though.

At the door is a beautiful woman, and I'm immediately jealous. She's model tall. A few inches over my own five-seven, with perfect blonde hair falling just below her shoulders. She smiles genuinely at me, and I'm unsure how to react.

"Can I help you?" I ask cordially.

"I'm hoping you can, actually," she laughs. "I know Gabe Dawson lives here."

My hackles immediately rise, and I'm a half-second away from slamming the door in her face when she continues. "I'm trying to reach one of Gabe's teammates. Grant McNally?"

"May I ask what this is in regards to?" I ask.

"Well, I think that's between me and him. I mean, do you even know him?"

"I do."

Her eyes widen, and she studies me before throwing back her head in laughter. "Oh my God, you're his sister. You guys have the same damn eyes! I should have seen that as soon as you answered the door. What are you doing at Gabe's? By the way, I'm Teagan."

"Hi, Teagan, I'm —"

"Cassie. I know. Grant told me all about you. But that was ages ago. When did you move here?"

"Do you want to come in?" I ask.

"Oh, sure. I'd love to chat with you about Grant —" Teagan gasps as soon as she steps foot in the house and sees Mackenzie. "Oh. My. God. Does Gabe have a kid? Did you and Gabe have a kid together? Holy shit! Fuck. I shouldn't cuss around a child. Do you think she can hear me? I can't let her first word be fuck or shit."

I throw back my head in raucous laughter. "She's still a newborn, so I think you're good with her not cussing just yet. And no, I didn't have a child with Gabe. This is his daughter, though it's not public knowledge."

"Oh wow," Teagan breathes reverently as she crouches next to Mackenzie. "Oh goodness. She is so stinking cute."

"I know. She really is," I murmur. Teagan immediately thought Mackenzie was mine, mine and Gabe's, and I'd be lying if I said I didn't want it to be true. Would others assume she was mine? That Gabe and I were a couple? I physically shake my head in an attempt to jostle that thought out of my brain. "So, what can I help you with, Teagan? You said you're looking for my brother? It doesn't make a lot of sense that you're here when you probably know both Gabe and Grant are on a road trip."

"I took a chance to see if one of the guys has a roommate, or girlfriend, who would know how to get in touch with them." Teagan looks uncomfortable.

"Did you reach out to Grant yourself?" I ask.

"I did, but we — well, we didn't end on good terms, and I assume he thinks the worst and refuses to call me back." Teagan looks chagrined as she waits for my response. "You didn't know about me, did you?"

"I'm sorry, I didn't. In his defense, Grant has never been one to kiss and tell. I only knew about a high school girlfriend because I saw them with my own eyes. I don't think he's told me about one girlfriend since then," I tell her honestly. My brother may be a complete dumbass for a lot of reasons, but he's always kept secrets well. And he's never been one to broadcast his relationships.

"The entire time I knew him, he never called me his girlfriend, Cassie. Unfortunately, I think I viewed the relationship as much more serious than he did."

"Not necessarily. Grant is who he is. And while you may think I mean it in a way that you have to accept him exactly as he is, I only sort of do. But I also mean it in the way that Grant is incredibly confident in his ability to judge a person, or a relationship. If he believed in you and your relationship, he wouldn't feel the need to tell people about it. Growing up, Grant didn't care what others thought of him, or his choices. Once he made a decision, he was confident in that. He wouldn't backpedal based on someone else's opinion."

"That's actually what I'm afraid of," she says nervously.

"Why? What's going on?"

Tears fill Teagan's eyes as she begins to fill me in. "I don't know who else to go to. They said they'd release everything if I talked to anyone but Grant."

"What?" I ask, a feeling of terror filling my belly.

"Someone cloned my phone. There are lots of pictures and some videos on there. Some pictures are just of me and some of Grant, but then there are some of us together. Whoever it is wants Grant to pay a million dollars, or they'll put everything up on the internet."

I stare at Teagan in shock. "And you tried to call my brother? And he hasn't picked up or called you back?"

She nods. "I didn't leave much information on the voicemail I left him because I didn't want to frighten him. Do you think I should wait until they're back in town? You're right. I should wait."

Teagan stands, and I'm confused about how that somehow became my solution. "I never said that. Knowing my brother, he'll be furious if you don't tell him immediately. When did they reach out to you first?"

"Last week," she whispers. "I checked the Wolves' schedule and saw Grant was scheduled to leave the next day, so I decided to wait. But they kept calling me. Then, a note showed up under my apartment door yesterday, and I freaked out. I went to Levi's apartment first since he lives close to me. I tried Jax's place, figuring he probably had a puck bunny staying there to watch his guinea pigs, and finally came here today."

"I'm sorry," I say, clearing my throat, "did you just say Jax has guinea pigs?"

"Oh yeah," she says, a watery giggle breaking from her mouth. "He has like five or six of them. One bedroom in his condo is devoted to their cages, and he has a huge setup of tunnels that connect the cages. It's pretty elaborate."

"I am never going to be able to look at him the same way," I tell her. When my phone rings with a FaceTime from my brother, I grin. "He's not getting away now!"

I answer the call and wait for Grant's face to fill the screen.

"Hey, Cass, can you do me a favor?"

"Uh, sure?"

"Listen. My ex-girlfriend called a couple days ago and left me a message that sounded concerning. Something is up with her, but obviously, I can't do shit while I'm here. Can you check on her for me? I'd never forgive myself if something happened to her."

"Sure," I say innocently. "What's her name?"

"Teagan."

"Send me her info. How long did you guys date?"

"About a year."

"Seriously? And you never once mentioned her to me?" I say with mock shock.

He shrugs. "You know I keep things close to my chest."

"Why'd you break up?"

Grant sighs. "I really don't know. One second, we were talking about moving in together, and then the next, we were breaking up. I honestly don't know what happened."

"Sounds like you miss her," I comment.

Grant looks off in the distance, waving at someone. "I don't know. Maybe. Gotta go, Cass. We're boarding the bus to head to the arena. I'll text you her contact, and let me know when you speak to her. Just be ... gentle. She's the sweetest person I know."

As he ends the call, Teagan takes a gaping and quivering breath as tears roll down her face. "He doesn't remember why we broke up."

"Do you know why?" I ask.

She nods. "I told him I didn't want to get married, that I didn't believe in marriage. And that I wasn't sure if I wanted kids."

"Oh, wow," I breathe. My brother might keep things close to his heart, but he's always wanted to have a family of his own. So I bet that hurt him immensely. "I was right, though."

"About what?"

"He may not have called you his girlfriend in front of you, but in all the ways that mattered to him, you were."

"That's true. Listen," Teagan says, jumping up and wiping her tears away, "I'll figure out something. Tell him you couldn't reach me. Tell him I hung up on you when you said your last name. Anything. Just don't tell him why I called him. Okay? Please, Cassie. Promise me."

"I'll try," I murmur as Teagan gives me one last smile before she bolts out the front door. Looking down at Mackenzie, I lift my hands up in exasperation. "These hockey boys are doing my head in Kenz!"

And that's when I get my first gummy grin from my favorite newborn.

86

Gabe

CHAPTER 8

The remainder of the road trip passed by in a blur. I continued to text with Cassie, including daily videos. Still, we had yet to further discuss what happened between us, or what could happen in the future. We returned home with five wins and two losses, an excellent record for such a long stretch away from home.

Our final game was a rarity — an afternoon game — allowing us to catch a late evening flight and get home in the early morning. Ideal? No. But it meant I got home to my girls a day earlier.

Catching myself grinning as I look in the rearview mirror, I nod affirmatively. Yes. Plural. Mine. Cassie is mine. Ten days away made me realize how much I missed her. Part of it was based on the help she gave me. I don't know what I would have done if I didn't have her at home to care for Mackenzie. But the absence made me realize everything I took for granted with Cassie, and some tidbits that make her so inherently breathtaking. Her messy bun when she slinks in to get Mackenzie in the middle of the night. The smile she gives my daughter when she thinks I'm not watching. Sorry, Cass: I'm pretty much always watching. I love seeing her array of eclectic coffee cups sitting in the sink beside my monotone ones. Her super sugary cereal on the shelf beside my healthier options. The growing stack of recipes she's been printing off for months down the road when Mackenzie can have solid foods. I knew I could fall for Cassie the night we met. But watching her fall for my daughter has been an exquisite experience I didn't realize I desperately needed in my life.

It's half past one in the morning when I finally pull into my garage, and I don't even bother removing my bags. After quietly closing the door behind me, I take the stairs two at a time, rushing toward Cassie's room. I carefully open the door, expecting to see the crib, but find the room curiously quiet. When I hear a coo and a gurgle, I chuckle as I walk back toward my room. Did Cassie lie about moving Kenzie's crib? Or did she move it back already?

As I push open my bedroom door, I find Cassie rocking slowly in the chair, quietly singing a lullaby to Mackenzie. I don't think I've ever seen such a beautiful and picturesque scene. My heart breaks wide open for them, and I realize in such a short period, I've irrevocably fallen in love with Cassie.

"Hey, you," I hear her whisper, and I find her watching me with a soft smile covering her face. I carefully place my phone and wallet on the nightstand, and shrug out of my suit jacket before walking over to her and crouching. "I just got her back to sleep. I think she knew you were coming home because she's been waking every hour."

I find my hand reaching for Cassie's face, my forefinger tracing an errant piece of hair down her cheek before moving it behind her ear. "Can I hold her?"

"Of course you can. She's your daughter," Cassie teases as she places Mackenzie in my arms. I look down at her cherubic face, so peaceful and serene, and I'm overcome with emotion. My eyes fill with tears before I realize what's happening.

"I can't believe how badly I missed her. And you," I whisper, not missing Cassie's sharp intake of breath. I turn and sit on the floor, my back to Cassie's legs, as I place the lightest of kisses against Mackenzie's forehead, then lay my head against Cassie's thigh.

"I saw the game today." I'm not surprised at her quick change of subject.

"Yeah?"

"Yup. It was weird rooting for someone other than my brother," she giggles.

"You were cheering me on?" I ask.

"I was. I saw both goals. Also saw the fight," Cassie whispers.

I chuckle. "Daniels is such a prick. I fucking hate that guy," I tell her.

"Grant doesn't like him either. He texted me from the plane and said he was glad you basically knocked him out."

"I'm not sorry I did," I murmur.

"I can't believe it's a five-minute penalty, though. The sport revolves around fighting, but it has the one of the longest penalties? It makes no sense."

"Mmhmm," I respond, my eyes closing as I finally relax for the first time since I left.

"I debated on ransacking your closet and finding a jersey so you could come home to find me in it," she whispers, raking her fingers through my hair. I let out a yawn and a moan.

"Every hockey guy's dream," I mumble.

"Gabe."

"Hmm?"

"Give me Mackenzie. Go get ready for bed," she says with a light laugh.

"On one condition."

"Okay?"

"You stay in here too," I say tentatively, awaiting her response.

"Can I be honest?" she finally responds.

"Always."

"I slept in here every night," she confesses.

I swear under my breath. "Fucking love that, Firecracker."

"Go get out of your suit," she says, pushing me lightly on my neck. I turn my head to apply the barest of kisses to her thigh, then swivel to hand her Mackenzie. Standing, I extend my arms above my head and stretch, which untucks my dress shirt. When my arms drop, I find Cassie staring intently at my crotch, and I'd laugh if I didn't fear waking up my daughter. I walk to the bathroom and get ready for bed.

When I finish, I leave the bathroom and find Cassie nervously waiting. "I never asked what side of the bed you sleep on? I've been sleeping right next to her, but it's fine if that's where you normally sleep. I can move. I can sleep in the other room, too, if you want to stretch out since you've been sleeping on crappy hotel beds for almost two weeks."

I grab her hand and drag her into my arms, burying my head in her hair as I exhale. "I said I wanted you in here because I want to hold you. I don't give a fuck about stretching out. I just want you in my space, Cass. Okay?"

She nods against my chest.

"I sleep closest to the door. You stay next to Mackenzie."

"Why by the door?" she mumbles.

"It's a protection thing. Gotta protect my girls," I whisper.

It's almost unnoticeable, but Cassie's arms tighten slightly around my waist when she hears me refer to her as mine.

I groan as my phone alarm goes off, then roll over and throw my arm over Cassie's form, yanking her against me. Burying my face in her hair, I inhale her floral scent, and a wave of peace settles over me as a few errant rays of sunshine scatter around the room. Cassie stretches, pushing her ass against my morning wood, and I stifle a groan as I move my head to suck on the side of her neck.

"Your daughter is right there," she whispers, but one hand slides behind her to hold my head in place. I dot kisses along her shoulder.

"Want to join me in the shower?" I respond, my voice husky and gritty with sleep. I feel her nod, and I smile against her skin. I set my alarm thirty minutes early this morning, intending on making Cassie breakfast before heading to a workout with Jax, but taking a shower with my girl seems like a much better option.

We both tiptoe to the bathroom. Turning on the shower, we take turns using the commode while the water warms up. Once I'm done, I find Cassie brushing her teeth, and she thrusts a toothbrush into my hand. "I don't do morning breath. Well, I mean, I did that one time you kissed me before practice, but if there's going to be kissing, please brush your teeth first."

I chuckle. "Noted."

As I finish with my teeth, I lose focus because my eyes find Cassie in the mirror, slowly removing her clothes. She gives me a flirtatious smile as she realizes I've stilled, the toothbrush hanging from my mouth.

"Gabe," she says quietly. "You're dribbling."

I immediately take a deep breath, inhaling some toothpaste, then gag and spit a mouthful everywhere. Coughing, I clean up the mess I've made before turning to find Cassie, with a hand covering her mouth, doubled over in laughter. I pick her up and carry her into the shower. She shrieks as we go right under the cascading water, and it's then that I realize neither one of us is naked.

"Gabe," she hisses.

"Sorry, not sorry, Firecracker," I tell her, yanking her tank top off before bending down to take her lips in a searing kiss. Cassie moans into my mouth as her arms wrap around my neck, and she jumps up to coil her legs around my waist. I push her back against the wall tile, and feel her stiffen against me. Fuck. I bet that's cold. "Shit. That I *am* sorry about."

"I'll accept your apology on one condition," she tells me cheekily.

"Oh yeah? What?"

Cassie gives me a wicked grin. "Make me come."

"That I can do, baby. How do you want it?"

"Hmm?"

"How do you want to come? Do you want my fingers in your wet cunt? Or do you want my tongue? Maybe you want me to take this glorious ass?" Cassie's breathing picks up with each dirty suggestion.

"Would you think less of me if I said yes to all?" she asks breathlessly, and my eyes widen at her question. I was only teasing about the last one. I didn't think she'd be game for it.

"Seriously?" I ask.

Cassie nods. "Definitely the first two. But that last one ..." she trails off, biting her lip for a moment before finishing, "I think I'd like to try that. Maybe. Not today, but we could work up to it?"

"I'm up for whatever you want to do, Firecracker. You're running this show."

"Oh, really?" she teases as she reaches between our bodies and grabs my dick tightly in her palm. I hiss, resting my forehead against hers. The wet fabric of my boxer briefs provides a friction that feels phenomenal.

"You keep doing that, and you won't get any of my suggestions," I mutter as her fingers deftly slide up and down my shaft, squeezing at just the right pressure to send bursts of pleasure across my body. When Cassie squeezes the base almost perfectly, I grab her hand. "Woah. I'd prefer to not embarrass myself right now, baby."

Cassie lets out a squawk of shock as I kneel with her legs still wrapped around my waist. Surprising her even further, I grab the backs of her thighs and hoist her entire body up so her core is at my mouth. Throwing her legs over my shoulders, I slide her thong to the side, and then I get down to business.

There's something incredibly erotic about feasting on someone and watching their reaction the entire time. I can't always hear Cassie's moans and sighs, but I can feel them. My body is so in tune with hers that even with the cascading water sound reverberating around the shower, I sense when she's getting closer. Sliding two fingers inside her, I find her G-spot and tap, tap, tap. Cassie's legs tighten to the point of cutting off circulation in my neck as her body bows off the wall, and she comes on a silent scream. I might die right now, but damn. What a way to go.

When Cassie grabs hold of my hair as she comes down from her orgasm, I'm unprepared for the shift in gravity, sending me to the floor. Cassie topples onto me, laughing breathlessly at the predicament we've found ourselves in. It just so happens she landed straddling me, my cock ready and at the perfect mark. All it takes is one slight shift, moving my underwear to the side, and I'm sliding into her. I begin a punishing pace, rutting into her with borderline hysteria, almost out of control with my need for her.

"Gabe," she whimpers, and I grab her head to bring it down to mine. Eyes open, I can't break my gaze.

"I know, Cass," I grunt as she moves her hands to my face, latching onto my hair. I can feel her walls clamping down on me, and when her eyes roll back, she lets out a loud, guttural moan, and it's the sexiest fucking thing I've ever heard. It breaks down the last wall of my heart somehow. I come hard, probably the hardest I've ever come. Cassie collapses against me, her pants hot against my neck as she trembles in my embrace.

"We didn't use a condom," she whispers breathlessly.

"Oh, shit," I swear. "Fuck, Firecracker. I didn't do that on purpose."

"I know. I'm on the pill. And it's not the right time of the month for me anyway."

"I'm clean. The team makes us get tested fairly regularly." When one puck bunny passes around gonorrhea to over half the team, it becomes standard practice. Fortunately, I was one of the other half that steered clear of Gono Girl, as we affectionately referred to her.

"I'm clean too. I haven't been tested in some time, but, uh ..." Cassie trails off, then giggles. "Well, it's been a while for me. You know. Since I had sex? Like well over a year. I mean, duh, not including you that first time. And honestly, I don't have much experience at all. I guess it doesn't really matter, considering I think you're still hard inside me —"

"Baby," I interrupt her with a laugh. "It's fine. I trust you. I don't care about your experiences in the past. I only care about *our* experiences in the future. Together. Okay?"

Cassie sighs blissfully against me. "Okay."

I'll remember this moment for the rest of my life.

Cuddling with the most beautiful woman in my shower, the individual tiles on the floor undoubtedly making huge divots in my back. But I couldn't care less.

I've got the girl. *The* girl.

I'm not letting her go.

Ever.

Cassie

CHAPTER 9

GABE
There's a box for you at the front door.

ME
I didn't order anything.

GABE
Maybe I ordered something for YOU.

ME
Ooooo, is it kinky?

GABE
That depends on how you look at it.

GABE
I should mention there's something in there for Kenz as well.

ME
Oh. I know what it is.

GABE
Do you?

ME

You're forgetting I have a hockey brother, Gabe. I know these things.

GABE

Alright. What did I send you?

ME

Jerseys.

GABE

And?

ME

There's MORE?

ME

You. Did. Not.

GABE

Those are ONLY for you. Don't you even think about somehow getting them on Mackenzie.

ME

Where did you even find panties with your number on them?

GABE

The internet is a vast place, Firecracker. One can achieve anything one's heart desires with a Black Amex and overnight shipping.

ME

Wise words.

GABE

Can't wait to see both of my girls wearing my number tonight.

ME

We can't wait to watch our favorite hockey guy on the ice.

GABE
Your favorite?

ME
Don't tell Grant.

GABE
Too late.

GRANT
WHAT THE FUCK, CASSANDRA

ME
Oh, shut up. Like you've never picked a puck bunny over me before.

GRANT
I've never picked a puck bunny over you.

ME
...

GRANT
That's probably a lie.

ME
It is. If you'd like, I bet I can go through my camera roll and find at least five examples of times you've made bad decisions with women.

GRANT
Let's not take that trip down memory lane.

ME
Probably wise.

GRANT

So you and Daws. I never would have thought to pair you up, but honestly, I don't know why. You're kinda perfect for each other.

ME

Why?

GRANT

You're both homebodies. Probably more introverted than either of you realize. But I think you're going to complement each other as well. You've always been a glass-half-full kind of girl, and he is more likely to see the glass as empty, or broken.

ME

Are you saying you think he's broken?

GRANT

No, not at all. He's a realist. Your head can be stuck in the clouds. He might bring you back down to earth while you'll show him how much fun dreaming can be.

ME

That was remarkably poetic, big brother.

GRANT

I have my moments.

GRANT

Hey, did you ever get in touch with Teagan?

ME

I left a message, but she didn't call me back.

GRANT

Damn. Okay. I guess she'll reach out again if she really does need something.

I hate lying to my brother, but I saw how broken Teagan was, and I want to give her a little time to come up with a solution. It probably won't do any good to tell him I've been in contact with Teagan, and I'm meeting her soon for lunch.

Gabe left me the cutest little set of noise-canceling infant headphones, and once I put those on Mackenzie, I can't stop fawning over her. I snap one picture of her gummy grin in the ensemble and fire it off to Gabe before we leave our house. Wait. His house. It's not mine. I guess it's their house. What's going to happen now? Am I dating Gabe? He's called me his girl, but we haven't clarified anything. If something happens that sours this — whatever this is — I better have a backup plan. I love my brother, but if I have to stay at his place again, I don't think we'll both survive.

Once Mackenzie is safely secured in her rear-facing car seat, we head to the arena in downtown Denver. Gabe gave me a special parking pass to park in the lot where the players and family park, right next to the arena, which is a significant relief. The thought of something terrible happening while I'm handling such precious cargo gives me a lot of anxiety.

Upon entering the arena, I immediately put the noise-canceling headphones on Mackenzie, as it's already loud. A quick check of my phone tells me they're still thirty minutes from the puck drop, but the energy in the arena is palpable. Gabe and Grant told me they think this is the best team they've had in quite some time, and they think it's their year to win the Cup.

"Ms. McNally?" I hear and turn to find a kind older man smiling at me. "I'm Shepherd. Mr. Dawson asked me to help escort you and

Miss Dawson to your seat. Is there anything you think you might need?"

"Uh, no? I thought I'd be in a suite or something, though."

"Mr. Dawson wanted you to be by the ice for warmups and the beginning of the first period. Then he took it upon himself to set you up in a suite where some other wives and girlfriends like to watch the games."

"Okay," I mutter. As soon as we begin walking down the concrete steps to the first row — because, of course, Gabe would have us front and center — I see a line of Wolves waiting for our arrival. Well, probably not me. Mostly Mackenzie.

The look on Gabe's face is priceless. I swear, if I let him, he'd carry Mackenzie around the ice a la *The Lion King*, and expect everyone to sing *Circle of Life*. The pride emanating from this man is spectacular. But then I see his teammates, including my brother, and they're all ready to fawn over little Miss Mackenzie in her adorable little number nine jersey.

Growing up with Grant, I'm well aware of how hockey teams become family, but I've never felt part of one ... until now. Each guy makes eye contact with me, and the ones I've met, Jax, Luca, and Levi, speak to me through the glass. When it comes to my brother, he winks at me. "Motherhood looks good on you, Cass."

"What?" I gasp.

"You heard me. You're beaming, little sister." He knocks twice on the glass, then pushes off the wall and skates back over to the bench, leaving only Gabe at the wall.

"Hi," he says with a lopsided grin.

"Hi," I giggle.

He motions for me to show him Mackenzie in her jersey, then swivels his hand around to have me turn. I do, but keep my eyes on him. I don't miss the darkening of his gaze as he stares at his number on my back. "Hottest fucking thing I've ever seen, Firecracker."

"Guess you'll have to tell me if it's hotter when I'm in only this when you get home tonight," I tell him sassily.

"Fuck," he whispers as he casts his eyes upward. When his eyes meet mine again, he says, "If you stay the entire game, ask one of the wives to take you down to the locker room. I'll shower as fast as I can."

I nod, then blush as Gabe's intense eyes don't falter. Removing a glove, he puts his hand against the glass and motions for me to do the same. I cover his hand with mine, then quickly grab Mackenzie's hand and put hers against his. Her tiny hand against his massive one is the cutest thing I've ever seen. Gabe's responding grin is massive, but I'm shocked at what he says next.

"I love you," he blurts out, then pushes off the ice and skates away backward. Gabe gives me a soft smile and a wink before turning to exit the ice. I'm silent, completely ill-equipped to process what he said. He loves me? No, he meant Mackenzie. He had to. Right? We've only been dating — or whatever this is — for all of twenty-four hours. Granted, we met a few months ago, but can he really mean it?

And why do I feel like shouting it right back to him?

This is insanity. I barely know Gabe.

But I know he brings me a peace I didn't know I craved. And his daughter is already such an integral part of my soul. I've always been the 'live out loud' kind of person. I wear my heart on my sleeve. I've blurted out feelings within a few weeks of dating almost every guy I've ever been with.

So why am I second-guessing my feelings now? Am I finally acting mature in a relationship, or is this the actual first time I'm in love, and I want to ensure it sticks? I settle into my seat as both teams exit the ice, my thoughts fully centered on the hot right winger who seems to have stolen my heart without me even knowing it.

It's been quite some time since I've fully engaged in a hockey game. Even when Grant traveled to Seattle, I typically couldn't find the time to attend his games. I forgot how I can get engrossed in the action. The crowd, which was loud before, has taken it up a notch. As the end of the first period nears, I can tell Mackenzie is getting restless. There's no way the noise-canceling headphones are keeping this racket out of her sensitive ears. I decide during the break, I'll go find the suite where the other wives and girlfriends tend to watch the games.

I giggle gleefully to myself. I'm an NHL WAG. That's something I never thought I'd say.

The game has been tense, with no goals so far, and there is a clear battle of defenses. According to my brother, Denver and San Francisco have never played well together. With only thirty seconds left in the first period, Denver has a power play, and I shout when I see that Gabe has a breakaway. I immediately stand and watch, my breath held tightly in my chest, as he fakes to the left, then shoots from the right. The red light above the net shines brightly as the arena erupts. Gabe is swarmed by his teammates, then immediately skates across the ice to stand in front of me. His grin is contagious as he stares at the two of us and mouths, "That was for you, Firecracker."

Mackenzie finally lets it be known that she's done with the noise and opens her mouth to scream. Gabe points up in the direction of the suites, and I nod. He blows a kiss before jumping over the boards by the bench.

Climbing the stairs, I'm immediately met by Shepherd, the gentleman from before.

"How did you know I was coming?" I ask when we get behind the stands.

"Mr. Dawson called to tell me you were ready to head up to the suite," he answers.

"They have a phone at the bench? Could you even hear him?" I ask incredulously.

Shepherd chuckles. "I've been doing this a long time, ma'am. I can understand the players most of the time."

As we board an elevator to the suites, I'm suddenly incredibly anxious. I don't know any of these women. They might be standoffish or obnoxious. Most of the women from Grant's time in high school and college treated me pretty abysmally in private but were nice to my face in front of Grant. I really don't know what to expect.

As soon as Shepherd ushers me into the suite, a woman is waiting for me.

"Cassie?" she asks, a southern accent appearing in my name. She's quite a bit shorter than me, with curly blonde hair, and she looks to be newly pregnant. One hand cups her tiny baby bump as she waits for me to answer.

"Hi, yes, I'm Cassie," I say, extending a hand to her.

She giggles. "Girl, I'm from Georgia. I'm a hugger."

I'm engulfed in a hug, and I don't even know this girl's name. "And you are?"

"Shit," she mutters. "Obviously, Gabe didn't tell you about me. I'm Hannah. I'm Luca's girlfriend."

"Oh! Gabe mentioned you to me, but he didn't tell me you'd be waiting for me tonight."

"I don't usually come to the games anymore. We've moved into Luca's house in Eternity Springs full-time, and it's about an hour from here. But Gabe wanted you to have a friendly face tonight, and he begged Luca to ask if I could come."

"Oh, that was nice of him," I tell her bashfully. Gabe certainly did put a lot of thought into things for tonight.

Hannah smiles. "He's pretty gone for you. All the guys said if he isn't talking about his daughter, he's talking about you."

I smile down at Mackenzie. "Talking about her, I can understand. She's pretty special."

"Give yourself some credit, girl. He talked about you before you started nannying for him. Luca said he wouldn't shut up about the amazing night he had with you and how bummed he was when he came back after getting breakfast and you were gone."

"Seriously?" I ask, my mouth agape.

Hannah nods. "You know how women gossip in the bathroom? Evidently, men gossip in the locker room. And my sweet man can't keep secrets, so I hear about everything. Her name is Mackenzie, right? Can I hold her?"

"Oh, of course. How far along are you?" I ask as Hannah carefully takes Kenzie out of my arms.

"About five months," she says as she coos at Mackenzie. My girl stares up at Hannah in wonderment, and I realize this is the first time she's ever been held by another woman. Well, I'm sure nurses held her, but from the moment she came home with Gabe, I've been the only one to hold her.

Wait.

I called Mackenzie mine, didn't I?

Oh my God.

"Are you okay?" Hannah whispers, and I notice my eyesight is foggy as emotion clogs my vision.

"In my head, I called her mine," I confess.

"And you're sad about that?" Hannah asks, her brow furrowed in concentration.

"No. Yes. No. I just really want her to be mine, I think."

"That's okay, Cassie. You've been the only momma she's known. You were bound to develop a connection and attachment to her."

"It's just ..." I trail off.

"You're worried about something bad happening that means Gabe and Mackenzie aren't part of your life anymore," Hannah states, and I nod. Damn. This girl is remarkably intuitive. "I don't think you should live life in fear. Who knows what might happen tomorrow? I want to live in love. I'd rather experience love than choose fear."

"That's true," I murmur as I watch Hannah loving on Mackenzie. "Oh! Do you know what you're having?"

"A girl," she whispers, a beaming smile covering her face. "But we haven't told anyone yet. And don't try to redirect, ma'am. I want the scoop on you and Gabe."

I sigh. "I think he may have just told me he loves me? But that can't be correct. Right? We've been dating all of a second."

Hannah smiles softly. "Luca says he knew the moment he met me that I'd change his life, and within a couple weeks, he was ready to risk it all. You can't put love on a timeline."

"I guess —" I'm interrupted as all the women in the suite gasp, and I look at the jumbotron screen to see Gabe lying motionless on the ice. I gasp and unconsciously grab Mackenzie from Hannah's arms, as if holding a piece of Gabe will either make me feel better or get him to stand up. The screen replays the incident, and I see a San Francisco player shove Gabe hard into the boards. When another Wolves player hits the two of them, all three go onto the ice. But Gabe doesn't get up immediately.

And that's when the camera zooms in on Gabe's face, and I see a sizable gash on his jaw.

Every person in the suite is completely silent except for me. I'm chanting, "This is normal. Hockey injuries happen. He's fine. Daddy's fine. This happens."

When I see Gabe move his arm, I sigh in relief. He waves the trainer away and carefully rises to his feet. I'm studying his movements, knowing exactly what a player will look like after a concussion. Gabe seems to be moving quite fluidly. He's ushered off the ice, probably to get looked at regardless.

The moment his helmet disappears from view, I have one hell of an epiphany.

I'm in love with Gabe. I *love him*, love him.

If something happened to him tonight, I'd be devastated.

Turning to Hannah, I don't even need to speak before she nods. "I'll take you down."

We swiftly walk to the elevator, and Hannah speaks quietly to a security guard. "Marshall can take you down to the players' area, Cassie. Can I get your number from Gabe if it's alright with you? I'm sure he'll give it to Luca. I'd love to have coffee or lunch with you next week."

"I'd love that, Hannah. It was wonderful to meet you," I tell her warmly.

Marshall gestures for me to enter the elevator. As we're descending, he looks at Mackenzie. "Gabe talks about her all the time. Both of you, actually. If I didn't know the situation, I'd have said she looks like you."

"Really?" I say emotionally.

He nods as we reach the floor and step off the elevator. "She has your nose."

I giggle, thinking about how amusing it is that it made my day for someone to say Mackenzie resembles me. I'm about to respond when I hear a crash.

"Are you fucking done? Come on! My girl is here, I need to get back on the motherfucking ice!" Gabe bellows.

"Uh, maybe we should wait a moment or two," Marshall says hastily, stepping in front of me. I shove him aside and move into the room where Gabe is getting stitched up.

Everyone stops when they see me, but when Gabe's eyes meet mine, I forget anyone else is in the room. "Did you tell me you love me?"

Gabe smiles softly. "You came all the way down here to ask me that?"

"Answer the question. Were you telling me or Mackenzie?"

I vaguely notice people quietly leaving the room as Gabe motions for me to approach him. He's sitting on an exam table, and it makes it so we are at eye level with each other. Gabe reaches up to gently move my hair behind my ear. "I was telling you, baby."

My eyes fill with tears. "Really?"

"Yeah. I love you, Cassie. I'm in love with you," he whispers, leaning forward to place a tender kiss against my lips.

"I love you too," I breathe. "I saw you go down, and I think I had this epiphany that I was in love with you, and I worried that I wouldn't get to tell you. Hannah got me down here."

"Babe, you know hockey injuries happen."

"I know," I say fretfully. "But it's never happened like this. When my heart was on the line. I don't know what I'd do if something happened to you. In such a short time, you've become my rock. That's really scary."

"I feel the same way, Cass. And I'm glad you came down to tell me that. But I gotta get back on the ice," he says with a chuckle.

"Crap. The game is still going on. But you don't need to impress me, Gabe. I'm in awe of what you do on the ice."

"Thanks, Firecracker," he whispers, giving me another quick peck before he jumps off the exam table. With his skates on, he towers over me. "You're incredibly short like this."

"I wish I had my skates so I could at least be back to our normal height difference."

"You have skates?" he asks as he puts his helmet back on.

"Of course I do. I wasn't about to let Grant do all the skating growing up," I tease.

"If you tell me you played hockey, I'm liable to request some extra time on the ice just to see you all geared up," he says huskily. I don't know if I'd call it playing hockey, whatever I did, but there were pucks and sticks, and I certainly could hit the damn thing. Just don't ask me to move at the same time. But Gabe doesn't need to know that ... yet.

I cock my head, backing up toward the exit, grinning mischievously. "I have a wicked slapshot."

I hear Gabe's deep groan as I walk out the door.

Gabe

CHAPTER 10

Three months later

"Are you sure your mom will be okay with Kenzie?" Cassie asks, nervously chewing on her bottom lip as we drive from our house. That's right, our house. I made it clear after Cass blew into the locker room and told me she loved me that we were together, and it was no longer my house. We're a family.

"You do realize my mom has raised kids before," I comment, a teasing smile on my face. I love how Cassie genuinely slid into being Kenzie's mom. She's so proactive about researching things and even argued with our pediatrician over something she felt was incorrect. But the kicker? The kicker was when she said, "I'll always fight for my daughter."

Her daughter. Not mine. She didn't even use the term stepdaughter. Cassie views Mackenzie as hers, and I'm incredibly proud of this breathtaking woman, and how she has become an integral part of our lives in less than a year.

"I know she's raised kids," Cassie says exasperatedly, slapping my bicep with mock anger while rolling her eyes. "But she hasn't been around our kid for that long. I'm worried Mackenzie won't settle down for her. Or that your mom won't remember the list of songs I hum at bedtime, or the order of the songs."

"I can't even remember the list of songs, Firecracker. But Kenz settles for me just fine."

"You're her dad, Gabe. Of course, she's going to settle down for you."

"And my mom is her grandma. Kenz will learn. And I fucking love that you say it like that, by the way."

"What?" Cassie asks, a confused look on her gorgeous face. I love that she's not wearing any makeup, and I can see the freckles dotting across her nose and cheekbones. Her hair is swept up in a messy bun, and she's wearing a tank top and cutoff jean shorts. I told her not to dress up because I wanted tonight to be relaxed. When she realizes what I have planned, she's probably going to be pissed.

"You called her ours, baby. Not mine. Ours." Grabbing her hand, I intertwine our fingers and bring the back of her hand to my mouth, kissing it. "Do you realize you're saying it like that? You've been doing it for a few weeks. I love it, Cass. I love that you consider Mackenzie to be yours, too."

Cassie is silent for a few moments before responding. "I hate that her mom had to die without ever getting to experience her, Gabe. I wish Nicole had lived so that Mackenzie could have another woman in her life to love on her. But I won't feel guilty over the fact that I do get to watch her grow up. And I won't feel bad for falling for you. You two are a package deal, and I think I'm the luckiest woman in the world for being blessed with you."

"Damn, Firecracker. Way to make me all emotional," I joke, pantomiming wiping a tear from my eye, but it's not that far off from the truth. Over the past few months, Cassie has become introspective about life, relationships, and parenthood. She almost always nails my feelings without me saying a word. Her ability to recognize my thoughts and know what I need ... it's mind-boggling. I used to think finding a perfect match meant both people had to be perfect, but that's not the case. Perfection is bullshit. But finding the ideal person for you is next-level. Cassie was made for me.

And frankly, I'm sick of her referring to me as her man. We talked at the start of the playoffs because she knew she'd be introduced to many new people, and she wasn't sure what to call herself. I jokingly said I would call her my woman, and she sighed in relief. "I'm too old to call you my boyfriend. It makes me think we're in high school or college."

First of all, I'm not old.

My knees disagree, but I digress.

I don't want her to call me her man anymore.

I want her to call me her fiancé.

"Did you bring me back to where we met?" Cassie screeches as I pull into the restaurant next to Cassie's hotel. I haven't been back here since we met. I think I knew I wanted to bring her here to recreate our first meeting and end it with a proposal. "Wait, do you want to role-play? Should we try to recreate everything exactly as it happened?"

As I park the car and remove my seatbelt, I reach over to cup her face. "I just wanted to come here for dinner, Cass. We don't need to redo everything from that night. I want to celebrate where we are now, but also think back to one of the best nights of my life. The night I met you."

Cassie sighs and subtly shifts her head so it's heavy in my hands, then moves so her lips kiss my palm. "I can't decide if my favorite moment of my life was the night I met you, or the night I walked into your house and met Mackenzie."

Some might be upset with that statement. How could the love of my life not choose me? But I know exactly what she's saying. A year ago, I felt like something was missing in my life. And when Mackenzie was born, that space filled up. But not all the way. Looking back, I can tell my heart pushed me toward Cassie, but I fought it. My focus had to be on my daughter. However, that night before my extended road trip, I knew Cassie was the missing piece. My heart was complete. I just had to wait for her to catch up.

"I think I knew the moment I held Mackenzie that she would be a significant part of my life. And then with you ..." she trails off, letting out a long exhale before glancing at me shyly. "I knew you were trouble the moment I laid eyes on you."

I throw back my head with a bark of laughter. "Did you now?"

Cassie nods. "Uh-huh. And for a brief second, when I saw you walking down the stairs holding Kenz, I was so excited. It was my chance at a do-over. I knew whatever had happened between us wasn't normal. But that first morning, when I woke up and you weren't there, I was so hurt. Seeing you walking down the stairs with a baby made me think you had left some woman to come to hook up with a stranger."

"I'd never do that."

"I know that now. But I second-guessed my own judgment when I thought you had snuck out."

"Can we continue this conversation over dinner? I'm starving," I confess as my stomach grumbles loudly. Cassie lets out a peal of laughter. She knows how hangry I get.

"Come on, grumpy. Let's get you fed," Cassie teases as she opens her door.

"Hey!" I shout, jumping out of the car and jogging over to her. "You're supposed to let me open the door for you."

"I know, but I'm hungry too," she says, her eyes alight with love and mischief. When Cassie's beautiful eyes sparkle, I'll do just about anything to keep her that happy.

Walking into the restaurant, I steer her toward the bar.

"We can get a table," she offers, pointing toward the quiet section in the back.

"So you can take advantage of me? I think not," I joke. In reality, the bartender has been saving the two seats where we met so I *could* actually recreate a good chunk of the evening. As soon as we're seated, drinks are placed in front of us. A beer for me and a margarita for Cassie. She looks at me, her brow furrowed in confusion, with one eyebrow cocked as she studies me. I bite my lip as I fight the smile that is aching to escape, and shrug in response.

I'm not surprised when Cassie orders her favorite meal. We don't go out to dinner very often, choosing instead to cook at home, but whenever we do, Cassie orders chicken alfredo. Considering almost every restaurant in the country has some version of the dish, I know to expect that order. She doesn't know that I always watch her take the first bite because she does a little happy dance every damn time. More times than not, the dance is accompanied by a high-pitched hum as she gleefully scoops up another bite. It's my favorite thing to see whenever we have a meal together.

I remember every detail from the night we met. Everything, even down to the outfit she wore. If it wasn't in the nineties today, I would have carefully laid out her clothes from that night to see if she took the bait. Instead, I discussed almost every topic we covered and asked her if anything was different. She agreed that Denver sports fans are rabid, and the weather changes every five seconds. She was still unprepared for how windy it gets here, but loves watching the sunset over the Rockies no matter the temperature.

As dinner draws to a close and we're walking out of the restaurant, arms wrapped around each other, I lean down and whisper in her ear. "Care to have a little walk down memory lane?"

As I steer her toward the hotel, she giggles. "Gabe Dawson, are you asking me to make out in an elevator with you?"

"That, among other things," I respond.

We swiftly walk past the reservations desk and grab the same elevator we used so many months ago. I, of course, take the opportunity to push her against the wall and kiss the hell out of her. I pick her up and throw her over my shoulder when we get to the floor.

"Gabe!" she squeals.

"That's not what you're supposed to say," I respond, smacking her butt.

"Oh, we're going for accuracy?" she teases.

"Of course, Firecracker. Chop-chop."

"Good Lord," she mutters. "Room nine-fourteen."

I take off, running down the hallway, skidding to a stop in front of the room. Bending, I let Cassie slide down my body, then turn her so she's facing the door. I begin kissing her neck as she shivers against me.

"Okay, we should probably stop. What if someone is in here?" she whispers.

"I'm pretty sure the room is empty."

"How could you possibly know that?" she asks.

I pull the key out of my pocket and wave it in front of the reader. "Because it's our room for the night."

As I push the door open, I subtly move Cassie, so she's further into the room. "What is flickering in here?"

"What? I can't see anything," I lie. It's battery-operated tea light candles. Obviously, I can't have real candles going when I didn't know when we'd be here tonight. "Hey, can you reach the light switch? It's right by you," I tell her.

As soon as she turns on the light, Cassie gasps.

The room is covered in peonies. Cassie once told me she wasn't the biggest fan of roses, although I have a couple dozen roses scattered on the floor. She likes how roses smell but hates how they almost always seem to die incredibly quickly. When I asked her what her favorite flower was, she got utterly glassy-eyed as she expressed her love for peonies.

So, I bought out the peony population of Denver. It took me visiting six different florists yesterday, and one online bulk order that arrived this morning at the hotel. I've got white, pink, coral, lavender, and peach-colored peonies. It's a spectacular sight, but my gaze is glued to Cassie. When she turns to face me, tears in her eyes, I'm already down on one knee.

"Firecracker," I begin, "I knew the moment I met you that I wouldn't be the same man I was before you. Every day, you remind me of how much of a gift you are. I'm humbled to be yours, Cass. I watch you with Mackenzie, and I know there isn't anyone else who could possibly be more perfect for us. You make me want to be a better man, and I hope you'll want me to be an even better husband. I'd be honored if you'd be my wife."

She laughs, a teary laugh that sings to my soul. "Are you asking me, or telling me?"

"Both."

Cassie bends down to grab my face, giving me a quick kiss. "Of course you are. I answer yes to both."

"Thank fuck," I breathe, standing and picking her up to spin her around. Cassie squeals as she wraps her arms around my neck. "I love you, baby."

"I love you too," she murmurs into my neck.

"Do you want to see your ring?"

"It doesn't matter."

"What?" I blurt out incredulously. It took me an entire month of searching every damn jewelry store in Denver before I found this sucker.

"I know you, Gabe. I know you probably picked a perfect ring for me, and I'll wear it proudly. But right now, I just want to hold you," she whispers.

This woman.

"Promise me you'll put it on soon?" I ask.

"Okay, but why?"

"Because I really want to make love to my fiancée when she's wearing *only* my ring."

Cassie shudders in my arms. "Oh my."

Oh my indeed.

Cassie

CHAPTER 11

I'm engaged!

Squeezing my arms tighter around Gabe's neck, I feel my body trembling with shock and adrenaline. I had no idea he planned to propose tonight. We'd discussed marriage, but nothing concrete. I wonder if Gabe waited until he thought I'd be ready, or if he chose to do it once the Wolves won the Cup. Either way, I'm so dang excited I'm marrying Gabe Dawson.

"Do you really not want to see your ring?" Gabe chuckles against my neck.

"Of course. I don't care what it looks like, though. I'll love it no matter what," I whisper.

"I know, but I searched for a whole month to find this one. As soon as I saw it, I knew it was meant for you."

"Are you going to put it on my finger?" I ask.

"I'd like to, yeah," he laughs.

I unwind my arms from his neck and step back to see him whip a box from his pocket. "Did you have that in there all night? How did I not notice?"

"No," he smiles. "It was over on that shelf by the door. I grabbed it when we walked in."

As soon as Gabe opens the box, I gasp, throwing my hands up to my mouth in shock. I was honest when I told him I wouldn't care what it looked like. Any ring coming from him would be beautiful just because Gabe picked it out for me. But this ring ... this ring is spectacular. "Gabe, it's gorgeous!"

He carefully removes it from the box and grabs my left hand. "I went to ten different jewelry stores. Nothing screamed you, Firecracker. I saw some pretty rings that I knew you'd probably be nervous about wearing because the diamonds were big. You aren't flashy, or showy. You're classic. Regal. Composed. This ring, to me, showcased all of that."

Gabe slowly slides it onto my finger, and I can see my hand shaking. "I'll admit, I know nothing about diamonds, or engagement rings."

"I didn't either, until I started looking," he chuckles. "The band is platinum. The main diamond is cushion cut and is around two carats. The pavé diamonds on the band add an additional carat."

"It's beautiful," I whisper.

"I also picked up a matching wedding band that fits the ring. I didn't grab anything else because I thought you'd like to pick out my ring."

My eyes whip to his. "Oh, absolutely. I'm thinking I'd like to match this one. Lots and lots of diamonds."

Gabe's eyes widen comically. "Uh, Firecracker —"

I burst out laughing. "I wouldn't do that to you. I know you, too, Gabe. You're not flashy. I'll get something plain for you."

His big sigh of relief echoes in the room. "Thank fuck."

I cup his face, yanking him down to mine for a kiss. Stopping the kiss, I say, "I do believe I was promised some lovemaking."

Gabe pulls my hand away from his face, and his eyes grow hooded as he stares at the ring. "I'd really like you to get undressed first."

"Not you?" I ask as I yank my tank top over my head.

"Not yet." Dropping my shorts, I'm left in a thong and bra. Gabe takes a leisurely look down and up my body. "Everything off, Firecracker."

"Can I do something first?" I ask hesitantly. He tilts his head to the side, one eyebrow cocked in question. Instead of giving him any more information, I drop to my knees.

"Baby, you don't have to. I know you don't like it," he tells me hastily. I've never been a huge fan of blowjobs, but whenever I go down on Gabe, I can see how much he enjoys them. So, I've made it a mission to get better at it. While I may enjoy reading books about women with zero gag reflexes, I guess that means I have one hundred percent gag reflex.

"I want to. Let me try, okay? Please?" I ask, peering up at him. When he doesn't immediately respond, I slowly unbuckle his belt. Gabe watches me intently, his gaze unwavering. I can tell he's incredibly turned on by how blown out his pupils are and his nostrils flaring slightly.

I pull down Gabe's shorts and boxer briefs, grabbing hold of his hard length and licking the tip. I hear his quick intake of breath as his hands find my hair, fisting the strands. I love how I'm at Gabe's mercy here but know I'm still in control. He's not forcing me onto his cock, or setting a fast pace. Other men might take advantage of me on my knees, but not Gabe. Right here, I know I'm in a protected space.

Swiveling my tongue around the head of his cock, Gabe lets out a loud groan. "God, baby. I love when you do that."

I pop off his dick and peer up at him. "You do?"

"Yeah. It's my favorite thing," Gabe mutters as I repeat the action. "There's this spot on the underside of my cock that is really sensitive. You naturally focus on it every time. It's fucking phenomenal."

I suck on the tip, and I feel his hands tighten in my hair. Feeling emboldened, I push forward to take in another inch, focusing on breathing through my nose. I've been watching some online videos with tips for giving good head. I'm not embarrassed by it. I want to make things good for Gabe. No, I want to make them great. I want to blow his mind. Pun absolutely intended.

When I suck exceptionally hard, I hear a guttural moan. Gabe's eyes are closed, his head thrown back, obviously in the throes of pleasure. But that won't work.

"Gabe," I say, my mouth still full of him. "Open your eyes. Watch me."

I make a big motion with my left hand, squeezing the base of his cock, and his eyes zero in on the engagement ring. "God dammit, baby. Your mouth is a den of sin. Those pink lips wrapped around me, and your mascara starting to water? Fucking beautiful."

I smile around him, but then I get a little too big for my britches. I decide to push forward with gusto, and Gabe's dick hits the back of my throat. I immediately gag, my eyes fill with tears, and I push him away out of fear I might actually puke. Coughing, I fall to the side.

Gabe immediately drops to the floor in front of me. "Shit, did I do that? I'm so fucking sorry, Firecracker."

I can't help but laugh as I get my breath back. Full belly laughs as my new fiancé looks at me with concern, for fear he punctured the back of my throat with his dick. "I was doing so well!"

"You were," he says hesitantly. "Not that you needed to. I certainly don't need a blowjob to enjoy sex with you, Cass. They're great, sure. But I'd rather get off inside you."

"You enjoy going down on me, and I want to return the favor."

"I really don't want to be puked on," Gabe blurts out, and then a look of horror crosses his face. "Shit. I shouldn't have said that. It was rude, right? You were trying, and I about blew my load right when I hit the back of your throat, which probably would have really made you barf, and I don't know how the hotel would view that kind of cleaning damage."

I'm cackling as Gabe rattles off his worries. It never occurred to me that I might vomit, but I can understand his concern. "I was fine until that last second. I would appreciate a little warning should you ever think you ... uh, might blow in my mouth."

Gabe laughs as he leans his forehead against mine. "I'd like to continue our evening, but do you need a break? Some water? A snack? Tylenol for your throat?"

"No," I giggle. "Just you naked, please."

He gives me a sheepish smile. "That I can do."

Grabbing my hands, he pulls me up to stand and then pushes me back onto the bed. I'm surrounded by flowers, and the aroma blankets the room. It's perfection. Gabe quickly pulls his shirt off, then pushes his shorts and boxer briefs down to the floor. He yanks my thong down my legs and chucks it behind him. Crawling over me, he takes my lips in a deep kiss. I wrap my legs around his hips, nestling his cock perfectly against my core. He easily slides in, and we groan simultaneously.

"I'll never get over how perfect you feel," he grunts as he slowly slides out. I brace for a quick penetration where I see stars, but when nothing happens, I open my eyes to find Gabe staring at me. "That's better. Eyes on me, baby."

It's excruciating how slow Gabe takes me. Every synapse in my body is screaming for release, but Gabe is going at this leisurely. I flex my calves and attempt to force him into a faster pace, but I feel him tighten against me.

"Slow," he grits out.

"Faster," I whine, and he shakes his head emphatically.

"I only get to make love to my fiancée for the first time once. I want this to last forever," he whispers, sliding both hands up to grab mine. Gabe intertwines our fingers tightly, placing them next to my head, his eyes never leaving mine.

I can see how hard he's forcing himself not to come. Sweat covers his face and shoulders, and his arms tremble as they cage my body. I know he's trying to get me off first. He always does, and typically more than once. But this time, just this once, I want to watch him lose control, and know it is because of me. My blow job skills may be subpar, but I can squeeze a dick inside me like no one else.

Kegels are a girl's best friend.

Squeezing my inner muscles, Gabe immediately stops. "What did you just do?"

"What do you mean?" I lie. "Don't stop moving, please!"

Gabe gives me a look, like he doesn't fully trust that I'm telling the truth, but continues moving painstakingly slowly. So I squeeze again. This time, he groans, and his eyes flutter shut. "The fuck …"

I know he's close. His eyes open, but his gaze is unfocused. He's muttering incoherently, his slow thrusts uneven as his hands grip mine tightly. I decide to give it all I've got, squeezing as hard as I can.

"What the fuck is that? How are you doing that?" he yells. "God dammit, I can't —"

He slams into me, hitting a spot inside me that only he has ever hit, and my orgasm sneaks up on me. I cry out as I come, trying desperately to keep my eyes open so I can watch him. Watching Gabe come is breathtaking; knowing I made him unravel is icing on the cake.

Gabe collapses breathlessly on top of me, panting as we both shiver through aftershocks. "I don't know if I should be mad at you, or ask you to do that again."

I burst into laughter as Gabe lets go of my hands, and I wrap them around his back. "I don't get many opportunities to blow your mind, Mr. Dawson."

"You blow my mind every fucking day, Firecracker. It still boggles my mind that you let me love you, Future Mrs. Dawson."

I gasp, and Gabe raises his head. "Do you know what that means?"

"Pretty sure I do, yeah," he teases.

"No, not that part. I'm going to have the same last name as Mackenzie!" I exclaim.

Gabe gives me a sweet smile. "I was kind of hoping you'd want to adopt her."

I think my heart stops beating.

"Baby? You okay?" Gabe asks.

"What?" I respond, the word riddled with emotion as tears fill my eyes. "You want me to adopt her?"

"Well, yeah," he replies sheepishly with a shrug. "You're her mama. I think we should all be one happy family. Don't you?"

"Yes, I do."

I never thought moving to Colorado would be the decision that changed the whole trajectory of my life. That a one-night stand would end with becoming a mom to the most perfect little girl and falling in love with the best guy I've ever met.

I can't wait to tell my brothers and parents that I'm engaged! Grant will undoubtedly take responsibility for my relationship and marriage. But with the drama between him and Teagan, I don't know if he'll bring it up immediately.

But I'm getting ahead of myself, and I think Teagan should tell her side of things, too. I have a feeling she'll be my sister-in-law at some point in the future, but I bet the road there is full of puck-sized bumps.

Gabe

EPILOGUE

Four Years Later

"Firecracker? Come on, we gotta go!" I shout up the stairs.

"I'm going as fast as I can," Cassie mutters as she carefully shuffles down the stairs. "Your daughter wouldn't pick which Wolves bow she was willing to wear."

"I gotta match," Mackenzie explains as she trails behind her mother. "Momma should wear one too."

"Not happening," Cassie says under her breath, huffing a rogue lock of hair out of her face. When she's finally standing in front of me, she gives me a beautiful smile. "I think this is the last game I'm going to be able to come to for a bit."

I rest my hand against her very swollen stomach, feeling my son kick my hand in response. My son. A phrase I never thought I'd say.

Cassie is currently thirty-eight weeks pregnant. In her words, she's had an easy pregnancy. Unbeknownst to her, our daughter tells a different story.

Every evening, Mackenzie gives me the scoop. Did Mommy cry

today? Did she vomit? How many times did she comment on forgetting something? Did she yell at all? Any weird food cravings?

Mackenzie truly enjoyed egging Cassie on once she realized Cass wouldn't say no to an odd food combo. A disgusting food she fell in love with was waffles, mustard, and maple syrup. The fact that I was able to serve it up without vomiting is a testament to my iron stomach.

"It's okay, baby. You hardly ever see me anyway," I tell her reassuringly.

I retired from the Wolves after finishing out my contract, and immediately took a job working for the team. I don't really have to work. I have gobs of money, and I've made sound investments. But I love the sport, and I love this team.

I first started out as an assistant coach looking at video of the team. I'd review games, compare stats, and look at future matchups to give info to Coach Davenport. But when our skills coach took a leave of absence for a personal matter, Coach asked me to step in. At first, I was apprehensive. Going from a peer to a coach seemed daunting to me, and I worried the guys wouldn't respect me. But I was so wrong.

As the skills coach, I fucking flourished.

Interacting with the guys and getting out on the ice is where I belong. I'll continue to do it as long as it works for my family. Fortunately, I'm only required at some of the away games. But the moment that Cassie says she wishes I was home more, or our kids tell me they really wish I didn't travel so much? Yeah, I'm done immediately.

"I know I don't see you, but I like being there to support you," she says quietly, placing her hand over mine. She winces slightly, and I feel her belly tighten under our hands.

"You timing them?" I ask, and she nods. Cassie has been having Braxton Hicks' contractions for a few weeks, but they seem to be closer together this week.

"Nothing consistent," she says with a pout. "I'm ready to have this boy of yours off my bladder."

"Yeah!" Mackenzie shouts, swiping at hair across her forehead, then popping her hip out in much the same way Cassie is standing now. "I wanna meet my brudder."

It's remarkable how many times people tell me that Kenz looks like Cassie. Not only are their mannerisms the same, but their eyes sparkle together. They have the same sense of humor, and the compassion they both have for humans and animals is unmatched.

Since Mackenzie's birth, Cassie and I have never shied away from telling Mackenzie about her birth mother. I managed to find some social media accounts for Nicole, and courtesy of connecting with a friend of Nicole's, we were able to get pictures of her when she was pregnant with Kenzie. We have pictures of Nicole in Kenzie's room, and our daughter knows that her mother is in heaven.

Cassie chose not to take on a full-time job, and instead has found charities and non-profits to volunteer for. She and Mackenzie both love to help at the humane society, as well as a local cat rescue. They promised not to adopt any cats.

So far, I've come home three different times to new cats roaming around our house. As if I'd ever say no to my girls, and they know it. Once they bat their eyelashes at me, all bets are off.

***

Two hours later, I'm so focused on the game that I barely hear my name being called repeatedly. "Daws!"

Swiveling, I see one of our equipment managers beckoning me out to the hallway. "Your wife needs to speak to you."

Cassie and I were married before my final season. Mackenzie was a beautiful flower girl, toddling down the aisle as she chucked handfuls of peony petals at everyone. Before I could grab her, she ran back down the aisle into Cassie's arms. With matching white dresses, I couldn't imagine a more spectacular sight.

Heading out into the hallway, I see Cassie with a tense but nervous look on her face. "What's wrong? Where's Kenzie?"

"She's with Jax's wife," Cassie states. "Gabe, my water broke."

"What? Really? Are you sure?" I ask, stupefied.

She rolls her eyes. "Unless I'm peeing in the slowest possible race ever, yeah. Plus my contractions are now coming faster, and they're getting a lot stronger."

"Holy shit," I breathe. "It's time."

"It's time," she agrees. "Kenz is gonna go to Jax's. She's stoked about seeing the guinea pigs, and we should probably be concerned that she's more excited about rodents than her new brother, right?"

I chuckle. "She'll have a lifetime with her brother. Let her enjoy the pig kingdom." Jax has an entire room dedicated to his guinea pigs. Elaborate cages, tunnels, and even plays music for them. How his wife accepts that idiosyncrasy is beyond me. "Firecracker."

Cassie inhales a shaky breath. "Yeah?"

I pull her against me, resting my forehead against hers. "We're having a baby."

I feel her trembling as her hands grasp at my suit jacket. "I'm scared. What if something happens?"

"Nothing is gonna happen," I tell her reassuringly, but even I'm a little paranoid. Mackenzie's mom had a complication after birth that ended her life. If something were to happen to Cassie ... I visibly shake my head, as if forcing the thought to get out of my mind. I won't think like that. I *can't* think like that.

***

Fifteen hours later, I'm in awe watching Cassie breastfeed our son for the first time. Max Gabriel Dawson came into the world screaming his head off. I wasn't too keen on giving Max the middle name of Gabriel, but Cass was hellbent on it. She said she wanted him to always have a piece of me. I argued that Dawson was a good enough piece, but she solemnly said no. Mackenzie has her mom's first name as her middle name, Nicole, and Cassie wanted Max to have a similar connection.

"Knock, knock," I hear from the doorway. Jax peeks in. "You ready for your girl? She's a little too excited to meet her brother."

"Outta my way Uncle Jax! My Max needs me!" Mackenzie yells, and I see her push her way around his legs. Carrying a bear stuffed animal identical to the one Jax gave her on her first birthday, my daughter gives me a beautiful smile. "Mommy?"

"Right here, baby," Cassie says quietly. Mackenzie's eyes light up as she looks around me to spot her mom holding her new brother. Without asking, she takes off for the bed, climbing onto it immediately. "You've been waiting a while, huh."

"Yeah," Mackenzie says dramatically, swiping at a curl against her forehead. "I've been waiting my whole life, Mommy."

As I stare at my entire world cuddled together on that uncomfortable hospital bed, I can't help but agree with my daughter. I've been waiting my whole life for this moment right here.

***

Ready for more Denver Wolves action? Sign up for my newsletter to receive updated information on future books!

Want to read how Luca and Hannah met? Check out the first chapter of their story on the next page, and grab Worth the Risk on Amazon/KU today!

Interested in reading about how Jax Mitchell finds his happily ever after? Turn the page for a sneak peek at Forecasting the Forward, available Spring 2025!

Sneak Peek

Forecasting the Forward
    Coming Spring 2025

Becca

"You're a great friend, Dani, but I think I might die if I have another blind date. Even if it's one set up by you."

"Come on."

"No. They keep getting worse," I moan to my friend, and co-worker, Danica.

If I have one more well-meaning friend or co-worker attempt to set me up, I may lose my mind. Here lies Rebecca Stephens, meteorologist extraordinaire, killed by too much small-talk, overuse of Axe Body Spray, and way too many dick pics.

May she finally rest in peace.

Alone, but in peace.

"Okay, but seriously, this is the one for you. I promise!" Danica says, gripping my hand between her ridiculously cold ones. Goodness, how are her hands this cold? We are sitting outside in August, where the temperature topped out at a balmy ninety nine degrees at Denver International Airport today. Courtesy of our studio being surrounded by concrete buildings shooting up dozens of stories, I'm sure our downtown temp is into the triple digits.

"No more dates, Dani. Really. I can't go on one more bad first date," I moan.

"They couldn't have all been bad," she says hesitantly. "You're the hottest meteorologist on tv here, and you're regularly featured on national shows. How could these guys perform so badly? Do you think they're all nervous because you're famous?"

"I'm not famous," I murmur.

Danica scoffs. "For Denver we are. The only people who count as bigger celebrities are the sports stars here."

I find myself grimacing. "And those are the guys I definitely stay away from. They think they're above everyone else, all cocky and self-absorbed. I have no desire to experience that day in and day out."

Danica laughs, her pitch higher than normal, and I notice her face reddens slightly. I chalk it up to the warm temperatures and move on. "Should I give you a list of why every blind date has gone badly?"

"Uh, okay," she says, looking behind me. "Sure."

I slap my hands together, rubbing them against one another as I excitedly list what should be a very bad list. Somehow, it's become a code for me, and it's almost as if it's gotten so bad that I don't think a man can give me a good first date. "I had the guy who told me his mother kept all of his hair clippings."

"Like ... as a kid?" Danica asks hesitantly.

"No. His entire life," I say smugly. Her face screws up in disgust, and I soldier on. "There was the forty-year-old man who lived at home with his parents. And before you talk about the economy, prices of everything, and saving up for a house, just know he'd never moved out."

"Never?" Danica whispers.

"Never. He doesn't even give money toward rent or food, and bragged that if 'things got serious with us,'" I use air quotes, "'It'd be totally cool to move in with him. In his parents' basement.'"

"Oh, dear," Danica says.

"One guy asked if I'd be a third for him and his wife. Another asked for him and his husband. They were curious, he said. They both liked my voice on television, and said I had nice calves."

"Both? The husband showed up?"

"Yup. Then they did the dine-and-dash, leaving me with the entire bill."

"It's a pity the network wouldn't accept a new piece called 'Becca Dates in Denver.' You wouldn't need to do any research," Dani muses.

"Which is why I can't do any more dates. I've come to the realization that I'm not meant to have a relationship."

"I promise I'll leave you alone, but only if you let me fix you up this last time," she says hopefully. I sigh in frustration.

"Can I think about it?" I hate hurting her feelings, but I'm so over blind dates.

"You know what?" she says as she stands, "I'll take it. That's better than a flat-out refusal. I'll see you back at the station."

After Danica scurries off, I tilt my head back, closing my eyes, and enjoy the warmth of this beautiful day. I know I'll miss the heat when we're dealing with hurricane-force winds and blizzard-like conditions during the winter months. Colorado loves to advertise three hundred days of sunshine per year, but they neglect to inform visitors and newcomers that the remainder of the year is filled with cold, snow, thunderstorms, and fog ... sometimes in the same day. I thought I knew what chaotic weather was like when I moved here for my job at the ABC affiliate. Growing up in Indiana, I was used to severe weather, snowstorms, and the kind of humid cold that could freeze the snot in my nose as soon as I stepped outside. Once I graduated with my degree in meteorology from Valparaiso University, I grabbed the first broadcast position I could find, serving the tiny market of Gulfport, Mississippi. Coming from the Midwest, I was thrilled to be on the coast, assuming I'd get to cover hurricanes every year. In the three years there, only one hurricane came close to Gulfport, and it happened the week I was back in Indiana for my grandfather's funeral.

After Gulfport, I moved up to Knoxville, Tennessee. After two years, I took a morning position with a station in Cincinnati, then moved again to Kansas City. When the morning meteorologist position opened up in Denver, I was thrilled to apply. I'd always been fascinated by the Rocky Mountains, especially how the topography and elevation impact weather. I've been blissfully happy in my position here for five years, and finally accepted the chief meteorologist position only a year ago. They're going to have to force me out of here.

I was meant to be a Coloradan. I find joy in every season, and I never miss an opportunity to gape at the mountains. Great food, shopping, and outdoor activities. The dating market, however, was dryer than a la Niña summer in Colorado. Any man I do meet shows his true colors within two dates: he's either married, a compulsive liar, talks about having an open relationship on the first date, or lives at home with his mom.

"He's as windy as a sack full of farts," Grammy used to say. My grandmother, God rest her sassy soul, was from southern Kentucky, near the Tennessee border. She grew up dirt poor. I thought that was just a phrase until she explained that the house she spent her first five years in didn't have flooring. It was literally just a dirt floor. One of nine siblings, Grammy fondly remembers her momma reading to them every night by candlelight, and all the fun she could have with her sisters with only the outside as a toy. "We played a lot of pretend. On the rare chance we got a new toy, oh my, we'd be happier than a dead pig in the sunshine."

Translation: they had fun.

Grammy taught me to find joy in the little things. Don't focus on trivial matters. Look at the big picture before writing something — or someone — off.

Which is why I'll let Danica set me up one last time. Her heart is in the right place, but I think I need a dating moratorium. A man sabbatical. A no sex semester.

Sighing, I grab my bag from under the table, and stand up to push my chair in. As I look down to see a new text message, I hit something solid. Gasping, I let go of my phone, throwing my arms out to balance myself. I already envision slamming into the pavement, and hope I avoid scraping my face. No matter what I tell viewers, they'll assume the worst. Or, they'll think I'm doing it for attention. I can never win, and usually get at least one hateful email per week about something. My skirt was too tight. Too pink. Too loose. Too bland. Someone didn't like my hair. Thought it looked like a hooker's hair. Asked if I owned a hairbrush. Have I gained weight? How far along am I in the pregnancy? Do I ever eat? I need to see a physician to treat my undiagnosed bulimia. Oh, and I mispronounced the name of a town in the south of France while showing a video of a flash flood. How dare I.

Before gravity takes over, a warm arm clamps around my waist, yanking me into the solid surface I bounced off. Another arm lashes out, grabbing my phone with alarmingly quick reflexes.

"Are you okay?" Wow. That deep voice, a baritone that I feel in my bones, seems smooth yet gritty at the same time. I have an immediate thought of that voice talking me through an orgasm, and I instinctively shudder. For fuck's sake. It's been way too long since I've had sex, and my lady bits are taking notice.

As I gather my wits about me, my eyes take in the body from the neck down. Athletic shorts snugly cover incredibly thick thighs, while black and white slides sit on his sturdy feet. How can I be thinking of feet as sturdy? I don't know, but this guy has them.

A loose University of Michigan t-shirt adorns a thick chest. It's a well-loved shirt, the large M faded in the middle, but the fabric feels soft under my fingertips. That's right, I'm now fingering his shirt.

"Oh! I'm so sorry, I wasn't looking," I stammer, pushing against his chest to step away. It's only then that I get a view of his face.

And holy hell, what a face. I should know, he's featured on the news almost daily.

Jacob Mitchell.

Star center for the NHL Denver Wolves.

It explains the athletic slides, as well as the tree trunk sized thighs that could probably crack a coconut if he tried hard enough. A backwards hat covers dark blonde curls that always look perfectly out of control, and I hate knowing I've thought about what it might feel like to run my fingers through them. I just know his hair is soft.

"You okay, darlin'?" he asks again, his stupid southern twang hitting all the right places in my body. When his grin widens, I realize he knows he's affecting me, and that really pisses me off.

I hate athletes. Loathe. Detest.

That's not entirely true, as virtually every long-term boyfriend I've had in my life has been an athlete in one way or another.

Professional athletes? Not enough words to express my disdain for them.

"Do I know you from somewhere?" he says, and I laugh sarcastically.

"That's the best you can come up with?"

His brow furrows as he studies me. "That wasn't a line. You look really familiar."

"I get that a lot." I'm not going to explain myself. He probably only watches the sports report on my channel, undoubtedly ignoring anything else newsworthy.

"Me too."

I roll my eyes as I push away from him. Yeah, he's still holding onto my waist, and I'm clueless as to why I've stood stationary this entire time. Jeez, Becs. Get it together. "Okay. Great. Gotta go."

I step back, and the warmth of his arm drops from me. Beautiful baby blue eyes peer down at me in confusion, I'm sure due to me not falling at his feet like women undoubtedly do. He reaches up to twist his ball cap around, giving me a glimpse at his tousled curls pointing in every direction before he slides the cap down onto his forehead. It's like his hat, when backwards, allows an open dialogue with Jacob. Once he turns it around, however, I can see the invisible wall slamming down as he schools his expression.

"You sure you're okay?" he asks again.

"Yup. Totally fine," I respond, slapping my hands together for an unknown reason. Am I okay? Hard to tell. Physically, yes. Emotionally, I'm a complete mess. This man has rattled me, which is something that rarely happens to me. "Thanks again."

"Hey!" I shake my head, choosing to walk swiftly in the opposite direction from where I need to go, but I don't notice it until my arm is grabbed and I'm spun around.

"What?" I snap.

Jacob chuckles, and I feel the sound like the lightest of touches wafting across my skin. "You want your phone back, or is it mine now?"

I look at his bemused expression, one hand extended as he holds my phone toward me. "Oh. Yeah. Uh, sorry."

"Also, Spitfire, I think you were walking that way," he says, gesturing with his head behind us. "Although it's nice knowing I rattled you."

"I'm not rattled," I lie. "I forgot where I was going for a second."

"Uh huh. Keep telling yourself that," he says with a wicked grin.

"I just got turned around when I ran into you. Maybe I have a concussion from hitting your massive body." Blood drains from my face as my eyes widen, and Jacob's grin gets even bigger. "I mean you're like a brick wall, and I probably hit those amazing pecs. At least I didn't hit your dick, and oh my God, I need to stop talking now."

Jacob throws his head back in laughter, and mortification covers me. Growing up, I had trouble with not recognizing when I needed a filter. It took years of working on communication, as well as a very long-standing relationship with my therapist, to teach me the social skills I lacked. One interaction with Jacob Mitchell has me reeling, and I'm spiraling as I think back to a tumultuous childhood where I never felt I got the support and unconditional love I craved.

"I have to go," I mumble, ducking my head as I dash toward the station. I hear Jacob call after me, but I'm too embarrassed to stop. I pop into the building next to our station, knowing there's a connecting hallway, fearful Jacob might follow me and do ... something. I don't know what.

Dashing into the first women's bathroom I can find, I collapse into the last stall, locking the door with shaky hands. A whirlwind of memories takes over as my breathing quickens.

How embarrassing can you be, Rebecca?
You have to apologize to the Miltons. You humiliated us.
I can't take you there! You'll say something stupid.
Why do I have to be stuck with the retarded sister?
Such a disgrace, Rebecca.
Shut your mouth before you say something ridiculous.

As the spiral threatens to take over, I hear a very distant voice reminding me that I control my own thoughts. My therapist, Simone, has been a light in the darkness for over a decade. She taught me years ago to focus on the present, looking at everything around me to ensure the past doesn't overwhelm me. *You got this, Becca. They don't define you.*

I take in a ragged breath as I take in my surroundings. It's been quite some time since someone, especially a man, threw me off my game so soundly. Simone is probably going to have all kinds of thoughts on this interaction.

Ten minutes later, my breathing under control and my skin no longer flushed, I make the way back to my cubicle at the station. I'm fortunate to have a desk by windows facing west, giving me a breathtaking view of the Rocky Mountains. Cumulus clouds build above the mountain peaks, sure to bring some late summer thunderstorms to someone along the front range of Colorado. I sigh, shaking my head in disbelief that I get to live here.

My usual gig is working the morning shift, but today I'm covering for another meteorologist for his afternoon stint. I've been up since just after two in the morning, and I won't get home until around dinnertime. My phone chimes with a text from my ChatBook app, and I find myself smiling as I look forward to whatever my online friend has sent me.

I hate dating apps. Hate them. The percentage of men who use them as a way to cheat on their partners, send unsolicited dick pics, blatantly lie about their lives, and treat women abysmally just makes me lean in to the expectation I'll be living alone with my cats for the rest of my life. ChatBook started as a joke, and it has never moved past messages. Maybe it's the fact that I'm completely anonymous on this app, using a stock photo of a beach for my profile pic, and never using my name. My username is NerdGirl1025. I'm careful about giving out any personal details, and have yet to tell StickUM92 what state I live in. The only reason I know StickUM92 is male is because his profile pic is of his feet at the edge of what I think is the ocean. Well, I assume they're his feet. Maybe they aren't. Maybe I'm talking to a sixty-seven-year-old woman who never leaves her dingy apartment in Queens and hates dogs. Whatever the case, StickUM92 makes me laugh whenever I read his — or her — messages.

StickUM92: I hate olives. Hate them. I honestly can't understand how anyone can cook with them, let alone eat a handful. I've always hated them, which sucked as a kid because my mom thought they were a food group, and put them on everything. Because we were a "you sit here until you clean your plate" family, I was forced to finish them. A few times, I got away with telling her I had to go to the bathroom, then spitting a mouthful out. She caught onto that real quick, and then she checked my mouth before I was allowed to leave the table. Mom knows I don't like olives, but just sent me a big box of various olives for my birthday.

NerdGirl1025: It's your birthday? Oh wow! Happy birthday! Sorry about the olives, though. I hate them as well. I can't even eat anything with olive juice on it. They taint the entire meal.

StickUM92: Right? Tainted. And my birthday is in May.

NerdGirl1025: But you said ... seriously? And your own mother screwed it up?

StickUM92: I know. My mom either forgot to send them in May, or she doesn't remember when my birthday is. Honestly, I'm not surprised by any of it.

NerdGirl1025: I'm sorry. That sucks.

StickUM92: It is what it is. I've never had the best relationship with her.

NerdGirl1025: What about your dad? Can't he help?

StickUM92: They divorced when I was five, and my dad died a few years later. He had initiated the divorce, and my mom was really salty about it. She's been hunting for the elusive happily ever after ending since. She just married husband number five.

NerdGirl1025: Wow. Five?

StickUM92: Yup. That doesn't even count the revolving door of men while I was living at home. We moved a lot as she chased one guy or another. I think I saw every small town in east Texas by the time I was a teenager.

Ah. He lives in Texas. Probably why he seems so nice. I have yet to meet a southerner who hasn't been cheerful and fun to talk to.

NerdGirl1025: Well I say you slowly give the olives back to her, or donate them to a food kitchen. Might as well make some people happy with the disgusting little fake grapes.

StickUM92: Fake grapes. HA! I'll think about what to do with them. Sorry for being a little down-in-the-dumps. Any interaction with my mom makes me grumpy.

NerdGirl1025: I understand. That's how I am with my dad, so I get it.

When StickUM92 doesn't respond, I turn off my phone screen. Honestly, I get grumpy thinking of any of my family members. My father and older brother were the worst to me growing up, but I've held a lot of animosity toward my meek mother for allowing it to happen.

I haven't been home in over a decade, and I'm not sure how long it's been since I've spoken to any of them. As far as I'm concerned, I'm the last remaining Stephens family member.

Acknowledgements

This was so much fun to write. This novella was originally part of a small series with other authors, but I thought it was the perfect opportunity to introduce a new group of guys all living the high life as a professional athlete in Denver. Y'all know I love when I can have other characters drop in for a visit!

I'd like to thank author Tamara Rene, and my editor, Brenda, for answering any and all hockey-related questions, because your girl here is somewhat of a hockey novice.

It's also imperative I mention all the amazing women I've interacted with this year in the writing group Quill & Cup. I don't regret joining a year ago, when I felt like I didn't fit in anywhere. Thank you for supporting me as I am.

Lastly, thank you to my husband and kids for putting up with me when I'm in deadline-mode, for all agreeing that I wasn't stressed enough, so I needed to get a puppy, and for the younger ones not realizing what I write ... yet.

*Also by
Jennifer J. Williams*

Forever Series

Forever Sunshine

Forever Yours

Forever Ours

Forever Mine

Forever Us

Forever Together

Eternity Series

Worth the Risk

Worth the Trouble

Worth the Vow

About the Author

Jennifer was born and raised in Ohio, but currently calls Colorado home. A lifelong lover of romance books, Jen felt pulled to write stories with older characters, because "old farts" deserve love too. Jen prides herself on delivering realistic characters that struggle with normal problems. She spends most of her free time within her zoo: two kids, two dogs, and two cats! When not containing the chaos, Jen can be found lounging on her covered porch devouring books on her Kindle.

Printed in Dunstable, United Kingdom